Noah

THE COWBOYS OF CALAMITY, TEXAS
BOOK ONE

LORI WILDE

KRISTIN ECKHARDT

Noah Tanner itched everywhere.

Weddings had always made him uncomfortable, but he'd never actually broken out in hives before. An unusual reaction, but then this was an unusual wedding.

His ex-fiancée was marrying his best friend, and half the town of Calamity would be there to witness it, but the real draw was to see Noah standing up as the best man, an object of pity—or scorn—depending on your point of view. The Tanner men were known for making a few enemies in their time.

If Noah was lucky, one of those enemies would shoot him before he made it into the wedding chapel. But in his twenty-eight years, he'd never been *that* lucky. Especially with women. They'd been leaving him since he was eight years old, so he should be used to it by now. It was the pity of the people around him that he couldn't stand. That was one of the reasons he'd offered to be Shawn's best man, so he could face down the nosy townsfolk.

What else was a jilted cowboy to do?

For six long months, he'd endured the unwanted attention and curious glances of just about everybody in town. Heard the gossips whisper about him whenever he ventured into his favorite diner or tavern. The day after Amber McNair dumped him, the neighboring ranch families had felt so sorry for him they'd even started a meal train, dropping off casseroles and baked goods to his ranch house for a solid week.

That's why he intended to stand up tall and proud as the best man, proving to friends and strangers alike that his heart was just fine, thank you very much. And that he wished nothing but the best for the happy couple.

If he could just stop itching long enough to do it.

Angry, red welts covered his arms and torso. That was the only reason he was still in the chapel parking lot with no time to spare before the Saturday evening ceremony began. He sat in the driver's seat of his blue Ford pickup truck, his white dress shirt unbuttoned and spread wide open as he rubbed calamine lotion over his bare chest.

After squeezing out the last pink drop from the bottle, he wiped the lotion off his hands with an old gray towel that he kept under the seat. Then he buttoned up his shirt and used the rearview mirror to put on his black tie.

Thankfully, most of the hives would be hidden by his rented tux. He did have one near the base of his right thumb, and another behind his left ear, but as long as he could refrain from scratching them, they shouldn't be too noticeable.

They itched like crazy though since he hadn't treated them with the telltale pink lotion. His friends used to tease him unmercifully about his aversion to marriage. He didn't want them to know that matrimony actually caused him to have an allergic reaction. Which was why he usually avoided weddings.

Until now.

It might be understandable for the bride or groom to get cold feet, but not the best man. Hell, he *wanted* to be there for Shawn and Amber. If for no other reason than to dispel the ugly rumors going around Calamity that he was a lonesome, heartbroken cowpoke.

He pulled on his black suit jacket, then heaved a long sigh. It was almost time to face the music. To Noah, Mendelssohn's Wedding March sounded like a funeral dirge. It was, in a way, since it signaled the death of a man's freedom. Hard to believe it had only been four months since Shawn had sheepishly asked for Noah's blessing to date Amber and he'd given it without hesitation, hoping his best friend since first grade would have better luck in love.

Now the happy couple were ready to vow until death do us part.

A cold shiver ran up his spine at the thought of walking into that overcrowded chapel. But what choice did he have? There were more than three hundred guests inside, all waiting to see how Noah would react to his ex-fiancée exchanging vows with his best friend. He'd have to stand up in front of all of them and not flinch under their eagle-eyed scrutiny. Nor scratch at any of the hives that were currently driving him mad.

He adjusted the awkward boutonniere on his lapel. The floral decoration of wild lavender sprigs and fresh eucalyptus refused to stay upright on his jacket. Sweat beaded his brow, even though the September sun hung low in the cloudy sky, painting the horizon with dazzling hues of yellow, orange, and red. He cracked open his driver's side window and gulped in a breath of cool Texas air.

It smelled like rain.

A moment later, his cell phone buzzed on the console. He looked down to see a text message from the groom pop up on the screen. Picking up his phone, he saw five words written in all caps:

WHERE THE HELL ARE YOU?

He glanced at the time. “Damn.”

It was six forty-five and the ceremony was due to start promptly at seven. The last thing he wanted to do was show up late. He picked up his black felt cowboy hat from the passenger seat and placed it on his head. Then he turned and reached into the back seat for the wedding gift he’d bought for the happy couple.

The sound of loud, screeching tires drew his gaze to his back windshield just in time to see a shiny black pickup truck racing out of the parking lot, taking the corner on two wheels.

The next moment his passenger door was yanked open, and a young blond woman leaped into the front passenger seat. “Follow that truck!”

Noah shifted around and gaped at her. “What?”

“Go!” she shouted, a high flush in her cheeks. “I can’t let them get away!” Then the stranger turned to him, her smoky-blue eyes wide and frantic. “Move it, cowboy!”

She appeared to be in her mid-twenties, and he liked the way she wore that rose-pink dress and those slingback heels. But the woman was obviously crazy.

"I'm not going anywhere," he said. "Except to a wedding."

"We have to go *now*!" She rummaged in her tan leather purse, blond curls spilling from the loose bun at the nape of her slender neck. She pulled out a narrow black cylinder and pointed it at him. "Don't make me use this."

He'd seen the effects of pepper spray before, and he sure as hell didn't want it used on him. Now Noah just had to decide if he'd rather endure the pain of the blinding spray or miss the wedding. It was a tough choice. Then he took a closer look at her weapon.

"Wait, that's hair spray!"

"Yeah, and it stings!" Desperation strained her voice. "So, step on it! My baby's in there!"

That was all he needed to hear.

Noah switched on the ignition, shifted into gear, then gunned the engine. The woman flew back against the gray leather seat as his pickup truck shot out of the parking space.

He pulled onto the street, heading in the direction the black pickup had taken and ignoring the posted speed limit. "Why the hell didn't you tell me your baby had been kidnapped?"

"It just all happened so fast..." Her voice trailed off as she leaned forward in the seat, peering out the front windshield for some sign of the black truck.

"How—"

"There it is," she cried, pointing as the kidnapper barreled through a yellow light into a busy intersection five car lengths ahead of them.

They were almost to the intersection, but the traffic light went from yellow to red.

Noah slammed on the brakes. His pickup screeched past the crosswalk and almost into the crossroads, just missing the heavy traffic streaming in front of them.

Thud.

The wedding gift in the backseat slid into the floorboard behind. *Crunch.* Yipes. expensive crystal wineglasses inside the package had to have shattered.

Noah winced and twisted in his seat to reach for the gift. Maybe it wasn't as bad as he feared.

"What are you doing? She's getting away!"

"I didn't have a choice," he snapped, his heart still pounding at the close call. "We can't catch anyone if we're in a three-car pileup. In fact, I'd like you to put on your seat belt."

"Then what do you want me to do?" she asked, ignoring his request, "the Texas two-step? You're letting her get away!"

Clenching his jaw, Noah leaned over and yanked her seat belt across her body. He caught the soft scent of vanilla and felt a tendril of her silky hair brush his cheek. From this vantage point, he also accidentally glimpsed the lacy edge of her light-pink camisole and a sweet dose of cleavage.

He mentally shook himself, then cinched her seat belt into place, just as the stoplight turned green. He hadn't looked down her dress on purpose, but he hadn't looked away immediately, either.

Some hero. Disgusted with himself, he floored the gas pedal.

He wove in and out of the thick, Saturday-evening traffic, searching for any sign of the black pickup. Block after block, he scanned side streets and crowded parking lots. His pretty passenger did the same, her gaze moving between the front windshield and her passenger window. Neither one of them said a word, the silence growing heavy and tense between them as time ticked away.

Noah couldn't imagine what was whirling through her brain. Someone had stolen her baby. She had to be terrified.

Ten minutes passed as they drove around the town of Calamity looking for the elusive black truck. Then fifteen minutes. Then twenty. But the kidnapper had gotten away.

Noah's hands clenched the steering wheel. His chest was heavy. Maybe he should have taken his chances and run that red light.

If anything happened to that baby...

"We lost her." The woman beside him sighed.

His gut twisted. He pulled off the street and drove into a feed store parking lot. "Look, don't worry. We'll call the sheriff and give him a description..."

"That won't do any good."

"Sure, it will." He parked his pickup in an empty stall, then reached for his cell phone on the console. "I got the license plate number. The sheriff will track down the vehicle in no time."

She bit her quivering lower lip. "You don't understand."

How could he? He didn't have a child. And since he definitely planned to remain a bachelor, he'd never know the depth of her heartache and terror.

Or the depth of her love.

At the sight of one lone tear trailing down her cheek, Noah tugged the teal silk handkerchief out of the front pocket of his tuxedo jacket and handed it to her. He wanted to do more. But what?

"Hey, don't cry. I promise to do everything in my power to help you find your baby."

"It's all my fault," she whispered.

"You can't blame yourself."

"Yes, I can." She nodded. "I screwed up. I should have known something like this might happen. I thought I could just live a normal life, but I was wrong."

Hmm, that piques his curiosity, but they didn't have time for long explanations. "What's your name?"

"Josie." She sniffed. "Josie Reid."

She was a Reid? He frowned, trying to place her. The Reid family had been among the first settlers in Calamity, along with Noah's own ancestors, but he'd never met Josie Reid before. He would have remembered those blue eyes.

"Do you want me to call Sheriff Kane for you, Josie? We need to report this as soon as possible. He'll get every deputy out on the streets and contact the state police."

She shook her head. "Forget it. They won't help me."

"The sheriff sure as hell will," Noah exclaimed. "He's a good man, and we're talking about a kidnapping."

"I've been in contact with his office for the last three days, but the sheriff's department couldn't be bothered. Now she's gone." Josie took a deep, shaky breath. "Who's going to give her tuna for breakfast? Or let her sit on a windowsill so she can watch the birds in the trees?"

He blinked. What kind of mother fed fish to her

baby for breakfast? Or even worse, let her sit in an open window?

"Who will check her for ear mites?" She dabbed at her eyes. "And make sure she doesn't choke on a hairball?"

He drew back. "Wait a minute. Are you talking about a real baby or a—"

"My cat. Her name is Baby."

He let her words sink in, still not quite believing it. "You mean, I skipped out my duties as best man to chase after a *cat*?"

"She was kidnapped!" Josie's gaze narrowed on him. "You're angry?"

"Damn straight I'm angry, but not nearly as angry as Shawn and Amber will be that I missed their wedding."

"Surely if you just explain..."

"Oh, right," he said. "I can just hear it now. Sorry, I missed the ceremony, guys. See, this woman jumped into my pickup and threatened me with hair spray because someone stole her cat." He swallowed a groan, imagining what every person in that chapel must be thinking about him at this very moment.

She lowered the teal handkerchief and blinked as if seeing him for the first time. "You're wearing a tux... and a boutonniere."

"That's right." He adjusted the lopsided boutonniere on his lapel. How could this woman have duped he. "You just hijacked the best man."

"Best man?" Josie leaned forward, staring at him in disbelief. "Why didn't you say something when I jumped in your truck?"

"Because I thought I was helping you save a *child* from a kidnapper. That seemed more important at that moment."

"Baby *is* important to me. She's the only family I have left..." Her voice trailed off, then she shook her head. "Forget it. I didn't mean to cause you so much trouble." She unlatched the seat belt, then reached for the door handle. "Look, go back to your wedding and have a wonderful time. I'll figure something out. I always do."

"Hold on," he said. "I promised to help you and I will."

She looked at him over her shoulder. "You thought I'd lost a baby, not a cat, so don't worry about it. I won't hold you to your promise."

"The one thing you need to know about me." Noah met her gaze, "is that I *always* keep my word." Then he thought about the wedding. He'd already missed out on the ceremony, but he could still show up for them.

"Why would you help a total stranger?" she asked

and narrowed her eyes. "I don't even know your name."

"Noah, Noah Tanner."

"Look, Noah, I'm sure you're a nice guy, but I'd better handle this on my own. Just take me back to the chapel parking lot and you'll never have to see me again."

He hesitated, then checked his watch. "Sorry, but we're going to have to sit here for just a bit longer. The last thing I want to do is show up at the chapel as everyone is leaving. That would really set tongues wagging."

Her frown deepened. "What does that mean?"

"It's... complicated." Noah had hoped that appearing as the best man for Shawn and Amber's wedding would finally put all the rumors about him to rest, but now everyone would assume he'd been too heartbroken to show up at the ceremony. Which made him look even worse than a jilted cowboy—it made him look like a coward.

He shifted uncomfortably in the driver's seat, barely able to stomach that thought.

"You stay here, then." She reached down to grab her purse off the floorboard. "I'll walk."

He stared at her in disbelief. "We're a ten miles from the chapel."

"I walk a lot. No sweat Chet."

He shifted his truck into gear and pulled out of the parking space. “Fine, I’ll take you back. You’re the most stubborn person I’ve ever met.”

She stared at him for a long moment, then her mouth curved into a wry smile. “Takes one to know one.”

Chapter Two

As soon as the words came out of her mouth, Josie wanted to take them back and judging by Noah's long silence, he'd taken her all wrong. The loneliness of the past few weeks had gotten to her, along with the shock of losing her cat, but it was too late to take it back now.

Besides, she might need his help, and that was something she never thought she'd admit aloud. At twenty-five, she'd learned the hard way not to depend on anyone but herself, but this time was different. She'd made a solemn promise and intended to keep it. If that meant roping in a big, stubborn cowboy to get the job done, then that's what she'd do.

It was dark by the time they arrived at the wedding chapel's deserted parking lot, with only a shimmer of moonlight shining through heavy clouds in the Texas sky. The headlights on Noah's pickup illuminated her ten-year-old, red Mazda Miata at the far end of the empty lot.

"Tell me that's not your car."

"Yes, it is," she said, trying not to sound defensive. It had been a long day and it seemed to be getting worse with each passing moment. Her car sat lopsided in the parking space, the driver's side back tire was as deflated as her hopes of rescuing her cat tonight.

He whistled low as he pulled up behind it. "Looks like somebody took a big knife to that tire and slashed it up good."

"That somebody is named Doris. I saw her slash the tire right before she nabbed Baby. I was walking toward the chapel when it happened. Then she grabbed the cat carrier out of the back seat."

"You didn't lock your car?"

She bristled at the question, already feeling so much guilt. "Of course, I locked it. But I left the car window open a crack, even though I wasn't going to be out of the car more than a few minutes and the temperature is mild. I never imagining anyone could fit their arm in there to unlock the door. Then Doris was gone before I could stop her. That's why I had to jump into your truck."

The fact that Doris had gotten away so easily made Josie's breath catch in her throat. Not only had the woman taken her precious cat, but she'd also stolen the cat carrier that Loretta herself had hand-painted to resemble an English Cottage.

Josie had to save Baby. Her sweet gray tabby cat was three years old, and they'd been inseparable since the day she'd rescued Baby as a kitten at that animal shelter in Austin. The same day her life had changed forever.

"Doris is the catnapper?" Noah parked his pickup behind the Miata, the headlights revealing every dent and scratch on her beloved car.

"Yes, Doris Dooley. Do you know her?"

He shook his head. "The name doesn't sound familiar. Does she live in Calamity?"

"She does now. Doris and her husband Miles moved here recently." There was more to it, of course, but Josie didn't feel like elaborating. "She must have been following me today, because I sure didn't tell her where I was going."

He frowned. "I have so many questions. But the first is, why in the world would anyone want to kidnap a cat?"

She didn't like his tone. "First of all, Baby is adorable. Second, she's the best cat in the entire world."

"I like cats just fine." He shrugged. "I've got a barn full of great mousers and believe me, they'd never let me put them in a cat carrier, much less ride along in the back seat of my pickup truck."

"Well, I didn't have any choice. We arrived in Calamity three days ago and I couldn't leave her alone in a hotel. Besides, I don't believe the Dooleys will hurt her. They kidnapped Baby for leverage."

Thunder rumbled in the sky above them and Josie shivered.

Noah looked at her like she was off her cracker. "Leverage?"

Josie hesitated. How much should she tell him? She'd met this cowboy less than an hour ago. She had no idea if she could even trust him or where his loyalties might lie. "It's a long story, and it's been an even longer day."

"You're right. Let's get your tire fixed and get out of here before we get caught in a downpour."

Lightning flashed in the distance, making the dark clouds above them glow. Relieved that he wasn't pushing her for answers, Josie climbed out of the pickup and walked to her car. She'd bought the used Miata during her college years and paid it off by working two jobs. Despite its age and wear, this car had been one of the few things she could depend on.

Noah followed her, knelt down beside the tire and examined the rim, running one hand over it.

"I've got this." She opened the trunk moved and

her suitcase aside before pulling out the spare tire and setting it on the ground beside her. "You don't have to wait around. I'll just put on the spare and be on my way."

"I don't think you will." Noah shook his head.

She rolled her eyes at the way he underestimated her skills. The skills she'd had to learn growing up without a family or a home to call her own. He'd probably run for the hills if he knew the things she'd had to learn to survive.

Noah was a big man. She was five-eight in her bare feet, but he stood a good six inches taller in his black leather cowboy boots.

A shiver ran through her, but not from fear. There was something about Noah Tanner that made her want to forget the only reason she'd come to Calamity. Forget about everything except the way he looked at her with those deep-brown eyes and there was an electricity between them she couldn't deny.

Josie took a step back from him. The stress of the past few weeks was getting to her. Taking a deep breath, she turned toward the trunk and retrieved the car jack from beneath a panel.

"Thanks. Bye." She waved.

"I'm not going anywhere." He widened his stance and folded his arms across his chest. "And neither are you, at least not in this car."

"Oh, really?" She closed the trunk, smiling that he believed he could boss her around. "Why not?"

"Because when Doris slashed that tire, she also hammered the top of the rim hard enough to make it undriveable. We'll have to tow it to a shop to replace that rim, and that won't be open until tomorrow morning."

Her heart sank.

She brushed past Noah to inspect the flat herself. Darn, darn, darn. He was right. The tire rim had been damaged beyond repair. She knelt to run her fingers over the battered metal rim, afraid to imagine how much a replacement might cost. She barely had enough money to make it to San Antonio.

"Look, it's about to rain," Noah said, his tone gentler now. "And I'm starving. Why don't we grab a bite to eat and figure out what to do next."

Josie wasn't sure if he was talking about her car or her cat, but it didn't matter. She hadn't eaten anything since the complimentary breakfast at her hotel that morning, right before she'd checked out. Maybe a little food would help her think more clearly.

"Okay," she said, then looked up at him, her old survival instincts kicking in. "Why are you doing all this for a perfect stranger?"

He chuckled. "Because my granny would kick my

behind if I left a lady stranded in a parking lot at night. Besides, I promised to help you, remember?"

"And like I told you before, I'm not holding you to that promise." Her stomach growled. "But I could use a bite to eat."

"Then let's go."

Thunder boomed above them, and raindrops hit the ground around them.

They dashed back to his pickup truck and jumped in. Noah switched on the ignition and the truck roared to life.

Josie welcomed the warmth of the cab as she brushed the raindrops off her face. She needed some time to think about what to do next, but guilt gnawed at her for going out to dinner at a nice restaurant while Baby was in Doris' clutches.

Today had not gone as planned, but that didn't mean her life wasn't on track. After she rescued her cat, fixed her car, and got matters settled here, she'd be on her way to a new life in San Antonio.

Then she could put Calamity in her rearview mirror and never step foot in this town again.

* * *

Twenty minutes later, Noah turned his pickup onto a long, gravel driveway.

The rain had stopped, but occasional flashes of lightning lit up the countryside, illuminating the pastures and fields surrounding them. He glanced over at Josie, suddenly realizing he wasn't itchy anymore. The calamine lotion had finally done its job.

Or maybe it was the distraction caused by the intriguing woman beside him. Or both. Either way, he was feeling much better now.

She peered out the front windshield, a puzzled expression on her face. "What's going on?"

"We're here," he announced, feeling guilty for misleading her. Then again, she had threatened him with hair spray.

"I thought we were going to a restaurant. All I see is a barn."

The large, rustic barn looming in front of them was painted a classic red and trimmed with white along the eaves and windows. The Dutch gambrel-style timber roof was sloped on each side, and scores of twinkling white lights outlined the arched roof, square windows, and the large wooden barn doors.

"It's more than a barn," Noah explained. "This land belongs to the groom's parents, and they turned their old dairy barn into a reception hall. It's large enough to hold up to four hundred and fifty people."

She gaped at him. "Are we at the wedding reception?"

"That's right and inside that barn is a live band with plenty of free beer and champagne."

"You've got to be kidding me."

The farmyard was packed full of cars and pickup trucks, but he managed to fit his pickup into an empty spot near the corral fence. "Hey, you were invited to the wedding, right? That's why you were at the chapel."

Josie just stared at him. "No, I didn't even know there was a wedding until I arrived. I'd just stopped off to leave a donation to the church that Loretta had asked me to deliver. That's why I left Baby in the car. I wasn't going to be in the church five minutes tops. What do you think I am? A monster? I'm not the kind of woman who would leave my cat in the car for the duration of an entire wedding ceremony."

"Loretta?" He scowled.

She said nothing and her silence made him curious.

"Josie? Who is Loretta?"

She waved a hand. "Part of that long story."

He took a deep breath and held it for a couple of beats. "Look, it's been a crazy day. We're both hungry and I need to make amends for running out on the wedding, so would you be my plus one for the reception?"

She blanched. "What? Are you asking me to be your date?"

He held up one hand. "Don't take it the wrong way, this isn't a date." Noah hesitated. "Here's the thing, the bride is my ex-fiancée and I think everything will go more smoothly if I'd show up with a date."

"Your ex-fiancée? Sounds like your story is as long as mine."

"Yep, she married my best friend after breaking up with me six months ago. But I'm fine with it."

Josie's mouth dropped. "You're... *fine* with it?"

He nodded. "That's what I said."

The longer she looked at him, the more he regretted bringing up the idea. The woman had made him miss the wedding ceremony, but that didn't mean she owed him anything. He just couldn't stand the thought of walking into that barn full of people all by himself.

"Forget it. Stupid idea." He switched on the ignition, then reached for the gear shift, cupping his hand over the knob. "I promised you dinner, so let's just head back into town and find a nice place to eat."

"Wait." Josie laid her left hand over his on the gear shift. The warmth of her soft palm rippled through him. "Let's do it."

"Huh?"

Her mouth curved into a mischievous smile. "Let's walk into that reception and convince everybody we're madly in love."

He eased his hand from under hers. "Now hold on. We don't need to go that far. I just thought it might be easier to show up with a pretty woman on my arm."

"Because you don't want anybody feeling sorry for you?"

There was an undertone of bitterness in her voice, but when he looked into her blue eyes, he saw compassion. "Something like that. Plus, I know for a fact there is a kick-ass buffet in that barn."

She laughed, breaking the strange tension between them. "Then what are we waiting for? I'm good at pretending, so let's go, cowboy."

Chapter Three

Before Noah could prepare himself, Josie was out of the pickup and waiting for him in the thick, rain-soaked grass. He swore softly under his breath and opened the door to his pickup truck.

Now, he was doubting this plan. He'd never known a woman like her before. What if nobody in that reception hall would believe they were dating, much less in love? Then he'd look like an even bigger fool.

She started toward the barn.

"Hold on." He caught up with her.

She turned and slipped on the wet grass.

He darted to catch her, his arm went around her waist, and he pulled her upright against him to steady her. The feel of her soft curves against his body took his breath and Noah realized just how lonely he'd been these past six months.

Her eyes widened and she let out a soft gasp.

"Thanks, I'm fine," she said, stepping away from him. "It's these heels. They're not made for traipsing around a barnyard."

He chuckled. "Have you ever been in a real barnyard before? Because this one's been cleaned up pretty nice. At least the only thing you have to worry about is getting mud on your fancy shoes."

"I'm a city girl, so no, I'm not familiar with barnyards. But I do understand people. So, if we want to convince your friends we're a couple, we need to make it believable."

"What do you mean?"

She smiled, then held out one hand. "Step one, hold my hand."

Noah hesitated, looking over at the barn and picturing their entrance. She was right. They couldn't do this halfway or nobody in there would buy it.

"Good idea."

She stared up at him expectantly, then finally reached for his hand, lacing her delicate fingers with his. She gave his hand a light squeeze. "Don't be nervous."

"I'm not." Noah wasn't nervous, he was confused.

This ruse suddenly felt too real. And Josie was a

wild card—he knew nothing about her other than her life seemed to be a mess. The last thing he wanted was for this situation to get any messier.

"Look," he said. "We need to set some ground rules before we go inside. First, let me take the lead and do all the talking. Second, we stick together so we can keep our story straight."

"We don't have a story and you seem a little rattled, so maybe I should handle that part. I'm pretty creative."

"No, I'll do it. I grew up around these folks, so I know the best way to handle this." He sucked in a deep breath as they approached the barn doors. "And third, we're not going to stay long, so all you have to do is smile and look pretty."

She glanced over at him. "Wow, I can't believe you're still single."

"Neither can I," he muttered. He squared his shoulders and opened the barn door.

* * *

Josie just wanted her cat back.

So, what was she doing in this barn in the middle of nowhere with a thickheaded cowboy who thought women should be seen and not heard?

Then she remembered that her current situation

was mostly her fault. She was the one who'd left Baby in her car. The one who had hijacked the best man before the wedding. And the one who had agreed to Noah's proposition when she was half-starving.

As usual, she had no one to blame but herself. But that didn't mean she was ready to give up and despite what Noah had just told her, she had no intention of following his rules.

When they walked into the barn together, they were met with loud music, louder conversation, and the rich, tangy aroma of barbecued beef. Her mouth watered and her gaze moved directly to the buffet at the opposite end of the large reception area.

She was impressed that a barn could hold this many people. Some wore suits and designer dresses while other guests sported a more relaxed style that included cowboy boots and denim blue jeans. The one thing they all had in common was that everyone seemed to be having a fun time.

As if on cue, the band finished the song just as the barn door closed behind them. A sudden hush fell over the room as all the wedding guests looked in their direction.

Then a flurry of furtive whispers filled the air.

She glanced up at Noah, who stood frozen in place. For a big, tough cowboy, he looked very pale under his black cowboy hat. That's when Josie knew she had to act.

"Noah," she whispered.

He turned his head toward her, his hand tightly gripping hers.

Without even considering the consequences, she leaned up on her toes and kissed him—right on the mouth.

For a moment he didn't move, then he leaned in and deepened the kiss.

They each pulled away after only a moment, but Josie's heart was racing in her chest. She stared into his eyes and squeezed his hand. "One more thing."

He blinked, looking a little dazed. "What?"

"I'm taking the lead," she whispered. "Just smile and look sexy."

He'd made a huge mistake.

That was Noah's first thought as Josie led him through the gauntlet of round tables toward the center of the large reception hall. The last thing he wanted was to create a spectacle at the reception, especially after his no-show at the wedding. But he could feel every eye in the place on them as he walked hand in hand with Josie until they reached the small sweetheart table where Shawn and Amber were seated.

He saw the newlyweds exchange a puzzled glance before with uneasy smiles. Shawn's gaze moved from Josie to Noah, then back again.

"Glad you could make it," Shawn told him.

Noah stepped forward, ready to offer his apology. "I'm sorry for missing..."

"Noah," Josie said, "I'm not going to let you take the blame for missing the ceremony." She slipped her arm through the crook of his elbow and moved so close to him that wisps of her blond hair tickled his jaw. "Especially since it's all my fault."

Noah tensed as he looked down at Josie. She wasn't following any of his rules.

"I'm Josie Reid." She fixed her gaze on Shawn and Amber. "The truth is, I have a stalker who slashed a tire on my car just outside your wedding chapel."

"Oh, no!" Amber said.

"Noah came to my rescue, even though that meant he had to miss your wedding ceremony. I don't know what would have happened if he hadn't been there for me." She gazed up at him, her big blue eyes glistening with tears. "He's my hero."

Noah stared at Josie, shocked at how easily she'd explained his absence. Or maybe he was still reeling from that kiss they'd shared. He wanted to kiss her again just to see if he still had the same reaction.

Then her earlier words came back to him: *I'm good at pretending*.

That kiss was for show. Just like this pretend date. And it seemed to be working because both Amber and Shawn looked as if they were buying her story. It was true, although she'd left out some significant details.

"Please don't blame yourself," Amber said. "We understand. We were very worried about Noah, but we never imagined something like that keeping him away."

"I really wanted to be there," Noah said. "You have no idea how much."

Shawn rounded the small table and wrapped Noah in a bear hug. "I know, man. I'm just glad you're here now." He took a step back, a wide grin on his face. "And that you brought such a sweet gal with you. How long have you two been dating?"

"Well..." Noah began.

"It feels like I've known him forever. We met and we just... connected. I've never experienced anything like it." She gazed lovingly up at him, then turned back to Shawn and Amber. "I guess when you finally meet the right person, you just know."

"Absolutely." Shawn smiled, then reached out to clasp Noah's shoulder. "You're good at keeping a secret, you son of a gun. I couldn't be happier for you."

Thanks." Relief flowed through him. This had been easier than he'd imagined. Shawn and Amber weren't angry with him. Just the opposite, in fact. He'd never seen the two of them so happy. "Congratulations to both of you."

He turned to Amber and leaned down to kiss her cheek. "I may have missed the ceremony, but I promise to always be there for you two if you ever need me."

"We know you will," Shawn said. "And we might just take you up on that offer. Amber's already talking about building an addition to the house."

"One thing at a time," Amber said. "Josie, are you sure you are okay? Are you safe?"

"I am now." Josie smiled. "Noah is helping me with my car. I never dreamed I'd find a man like him."

"Oh, that is so sweet!" Amber placed one hand over her heart. "I'm so glad you found each other."

"We feel the same way," Josie told her. "And I have to say, you look stunning in that gown. Where did you find it?"

As Josie and Amber chatted about the wedding gown, Noah stared at them, a little stunned at how this had all unfolded. Then he glanced around him, noticing many of the guests weren't watching him anymore. Had it really been this easy?

"Noah?"

He blinked. "What?"

Josie smiled. "I know you want to dance with the bride, so now seems like the perfect time. Maybe I can talk the groom into showing me the way to the buffet."

"My pleasure." Shawn grinned at Noah as he led Josie away.

Noah turned to Amber as the band played "Unchained Melody". "You don't have to dance with me. I know it's... awkward."

"Awkward?" She put one hand on his arm and steered him toward the dance floor. "I think it sounds like the perfect way to put all these busybodies in their place. I'm so tired of the whispers and gossip about us. Aren't you?"

He gaped at her as they took the dance floor and swayed to the music. She and Shawn had seemed so happy these past few months. It had never occurred to him that Amber might have been caught in the fallout of their broken engagement, too.

"I'm very tired of it. Maybe now the Nosy Parkers will start minding their own business."

She laughed. "I guess there's a first time for everything. Although, I'm sure there will be plenty of gossip about you and the mysterious blonde. I had no idea you've been dating someone."

"I don't kiss and tell," he said, eager to change the

subject before he gave himself away. "By the way, I'm glad you broke up with me."

She looked up at him in surprise. "Really?"

He nodded. "I can see you and Shawn belong together. He'll make you happy."

"You made me happy, too. You just weren't in love with me."

"What?" Taken aback, he almost stepped on her toes. "We dated for a year before I proposed. We never argued and always had fun together."

She smiled. "That's called friendship. You loved spending time with me, but you weren't *in love* with me. We're friends, Noah. And my hope is that you find someone you *can* fall in love with." Amber nodded toward Josie. "Maybe it's her."

Noah looked in that direction, surprised and a little nervous to see Josie was eating a plate of barbecue while in an animated conversation with his granny.

"Or maybe I'm just happier alone," he said. "Like my dad was."

The music came to an end before she could reply. Amber reached out and hugged him, her cheek resting on his chest. "I'll always love you, Noah."

"As a friend?"

She stepped away far enough to smile up at him. "As one of my best friends." She turned to Shawn and stepped into her husband's arms.

"I better go rescue Josie again," Noah said. "Congratulations, you two."

Shawn reached out and shook his hand. "Don't be a stranger. You're welcome at our place anytime."

"I'll hold you to that." Noah left the newlyweds on the dance floor, feeling an odd sense of freedom.

He started toward Josie's table, but he got waylaid by friends and neighbors. They exchanged small talk and made jokes, and he felt more at ease around them than he had in months.

And he had Josie to thank for it. When he finally broke away from the crowd, Noah moved toward the bar, planning to grab a drink for both of them when he heard a familiar voice behind him.

"There you are!"

Noah turned around to see his granny. She was just over five feet tall and wore a green silk dress, along with sensible shoes. Her snow-white hair was pulled back into a neat French braid.

"I like Josie," she said. "I think she's good for you."

He stifled a groan. Noah had been afraid his granny might have that reaction when he showed up with a date. She'd been so distraught after his breakup with Amber, he didn't want to disappoint her again. "Josie is nice, but you just met her."

"I know, but I have a sixth sense about these things."

He laughed, then shook his head. "I'm sorry, Granny, but I don't believe in your magical powers. Besides, I'm not ready to get serious with anyone."

"If you say so." She patted his arm. "Just don't be afraid to take a chance again. I don't like the idea of you rattling around in that big ranch house all by yourself."

"I'll keep that in mind," he said, wanting to let her down easy. She worried too much about him. He looked around the barn. "Where did Josie go?"

Granny hitched her thumb toward the barn doors. "She got a text. The girl took one look at her phone and ran outside." A twinkle lit her shrewd green eyes. "Maybe you'd better make your move in case it's from another fella."

"Thanks for the advice, Granny. I don't know what I'd do without you."

"Neither do I." She placed one thin hand on his shoulder and gently pushed him toward the doors. "Now go after her before it's too late."

He laughed, then leaned down to kiss her cheek before heading outside to see Josie.

But she was nowhere to be found.

Josie trudged along the corral fence, wishing she'd worn different shoes. Her heels kept sinking into the wet soil and she'd almost fallen twice. There was just enough moon peeking through the clouds to light her path as she disappeared into the dark night.

She'd never felt so alone.

When she reached the end of the corral fence, she kept walking, wanting to be certain the wedding guests clustered in groups outside the barn couldn't see or hear her. She tried to ignore the twinge of guilt at abandoning Noah without a word, but she'd barely made it out of the wedding reception without bursting into tears—which would have certainly ruined the image he'd wanted them to project as a happy couple.

And they'd actually pulled it off.

She'd watched Noah dance with the bride while

savoring barbecued brisket. Amber was not only beautiful, but sweet. She had no doubt that Noah was still in love with her. Josie had never been in love like that, and maybe she didn't deserve to be. Not after putting her cat in jeopardy.

She finally stopped and glanced over her shoulder, the barn lights now just tiny, bright pinpricks in the distance. She kicked off her heels with a soft moan of relief, relishing the sensation of the cool, damp grass against the soles of her aching bare feet.

Josie couldn't imagine what Noah's sweet grandmother must have thought when she'd suddenly disappeared—or Noah himself, for that matter. She was supposed to be by his side at this reception, continuing the fiction that they were a devoted couple. But the only love she was feeling tonight was for Baby. She closed her eyes and took a deep breath, not letting herself imagine the worst.

She reached into her purse and pulled out her cell phone. The text message from Doris was still on the front screen.

> Call me. I have news about the feline.

Her heart pounded, and she fought to catch her breath. Panic had fueled her long walk and now it was overtaking her.

"Get it together," she muttered. "Baby is fine."

There would be no reason for Doris to hurt her cat. She and Baby had each been in worse situations before and survived and they'd make it through this one too. No matter what Josie had to do to rescue her cat.

A lone coyote howled in the distance, and for some odd reason, the sound calmed her. She needed to remain calm to deal with someone like Doris.

"You can do this," she whispered.

Josie hardened her resolve, then brought up Doris' number on her phone. Her index finger hovered above it, but she wondered if she needed to give this more thought.

If Doris made an actual threat to her or to Baby during the call, then the sheriff's office might finally be able to do something. Quickly finding the voice recorder app on her phone, she turned it on. Then she activated the speaker on her phone before she called Doris, so the recorder would pick up their conversation.

The phone rang twice, the sound eerily loud in the silence surrounding her.

Doris answered on the third ring. "Well, it's about time. I was beginning to wonder if you even cared about your cat. Of course, you missed out on the normal bonding experiences as a child, so nothing you do would surprise me."

Josie tensed but didn't take the bait. "Is my cat all right?"

"She's settled in here very nicely and seems to feel right at home. Thank you so much for letting us keep her while you get affairs in order."

"You took her from me," Josie said. "And I want her back immediately."

Doris grunted. "Poor Loretta. She passed away so suddenly and before she had a chance to let me review her new will. Did you know I used to work as a paralegal?"

"What do you want?" Josie asked.

"You know very well what I want," Doris said, her voice as sweet as honey. "To see that new will Loretta wrote and signed—no doubt under duress—right before she died. If you allow me to review her will, without any fuss, then afterward we'll have a glass of sweet tea together while you reunite with your cat."

"And if I don't give you the will?"

"Then we can do this the hard way and take it to court, but I should warn you that judges around here don't take kindly to folks exerting undue influence on the elderly. Especially someone like you."

"Let me get this straight," Josie said, still unable to

believe she was even having this conversation. "You're holding my cat for ransom?"

"Of course not," Doris said evenly. "That would be illegal. I've taken Baby into protective custody. A woman like you isn't a good influence on an impressionable kitty. You even abandoned her in the back seat of a car."

Josie closed her eyes, a sense of dread enveloping her. "You can't do this."

"I already did." Doris cackled. "And just so you understand, your troubles are just beginning if you don't do the right thing."

"Loretta loved you and Miles," Josie said. "She loved Baby and she even loved someone like me. All I want to do is honor her last wishes."

A sharp laugh carried over the phone's speaker. "Love? You don't know anything about love. You used Loretta. You lived in her house, ate her food, and even stole her last name. But that doesn't make you family."

"I never claimed to be," Josie said, squaring her shoulders. "And you've got it all wrong."

"Baloney," Doris snapped. "That's just another one of your lies. But here's the truth. If you want your cat, then bring me Loretta's last will and testament. If you don't, you'll be sorry you ever stepped foot in Calamity."

The call ended abruptly. Josie just stared at her

phone, then she slowly pressed one finger on the screen to turn off the recorder.

"Problems?" said a deep voice behind her.

Josie gasped, then spun around to see Noah emerge out of the darkness. "What are you doing here?"

"I was going to ask you the same question, but that phone call explains... quite a bit."

She shook her head. "You don't understand."

"You're the one who doesn't understand. When I couldn't find you, I was afraid that maniac might have taken you too. What did you think I was going to do when you disappeared? Just dance the night away?"

"I didn't think about that," Josie breathed. Aside from Loretta, nobody had ever worried about her before. "After Doris texted me, I just wanted to get away from the crowd and the noise." She looked around, realizing how isolated they really were out here. "How did you find me?"

"I've always been good at tracking critters and it's dark enough out here that it was easy to see the glow of your cell phone screen." He narrowed his gaze. "I still have questions. And the first one is, what are you *really* doing in Calamity?"

Josie hesitated, fighting the urge to confide everything to him. Her grief. Her fear. Her loneliness. But she'd always kept that part of herself locked up tight—

aware that revealing it would only make her more vulnerable.

That phone call with Doris had rattled her and even though she'd recorded it, now she worried that going to the police might endanger Baby. She couldn't take that chance, but maybe she could take a chance on Noah. "It's going to sound weird."

"I can deal with weird." His face relaxed into a smile. "Weird runs in my family, so you won't scare me off if that's what you're afraid of."

"I'm serious. It could get... dangerous."

He took a step closer. "Look, I'm already involved. I missed the wedding ceremony because I had to rescue my girlfriend from a stalker, according to the story you told in that barn."

"I know, but..."

"And that hot kiss between the two of us convinced everyone at the reception, including my friends and family, that we're a couple."

"Maybe that was a mistake."

"That's why it concerns me that my *girlfriend* is not only being blackmailed, but also threatened with a lawsuit."

Josie opened her mouth, and then closed it again. Because it was clear Noah still had more to say and she owed him that much after everything she'd put him through today.

"Because in a small town like this, news spreads like wildfire. And I've already heard enough gossip about me to last a lifetime. So, I'm not only on your side, but I will do everything in my power to get you and your cat out of Calamity as quickly as possible."

Josie wasn't surprised Noah wanted to get rid of her, but his words still stung a bit. "How much of that phone call did you overhear?"

"Enough." He searched her face. "Look, I don't care what secrets you might have. I have secrets, too. But I can't help you if I don't know what's going on."

"Okay, I'll give you the short version." Josie sucked in a deep breath. "Three years ago, I met a woman named Loretta Reid at an animal shelter in Austin. I worked there part-time while finishing my master's degree in history. She was retired and volunteered there. We both bonded over the same kitten."

"Baby?"

She nodded. "The kitten was very attached to me, so Loretta offered to bring us both home. She had a room to rent, and she knew I was looking for a new place to live after my roommate got married."

"You took a risk."

"Yes and it was actually the best time of my life." She sighed wistfully. "I never knew my parents and I grew up in foster care. I changed families several times, never quite fitting in anywhere, but living with Loretta was different. For the first time in my life, I felt like I really belonged. Like I had a real family. I rescued Baby, but Loretta really rescued me." She blinked back the tears welling in her eyes. "Loretta passed away six weeks ago after a sudden illness."

"I'm so sorry."

She shrugged. "There's more to the story. You see, Loretta is originally from Calamity and still has a second home here. Her great-nephew is Miles Dooley. He's her last surviving kin, so he and Doris were expecting to inherit Loretta's sizable estate after she passed away."

"Expecting to inherit? Did that change?"

"Loretta made a new will. She told me about it the day before she passed away and made me promise I would take it to her lawyer in Calamity. She'd gotten ill before she'd had a chance to do it herself."

"Just to be clear," he said slowly, "Doris stole your cat so she could blackmail you into handing over Loretta Reid's new will?"

She nodded. "I think Doris wants to destroy it. They were staying with us in Austin when it happened. Loretta told all of us she made a new will, but not why or what was in it." Josie gulped back tears. "What's so odd is that Miles could still be the sole beneficiary of the new will. Perhaps Loretta just made minor changes or gave some of her money to a charity, like the animal shelter or the church she asked me to leave her donation with."

"You don't know?" His brow furrowed. "Can't you just read it and find out?"

"I would but I don't have it. And that's how we get to the wildest part of all." She met his gaze. "The new will is in Loretta's house, here in Calamity, where Doris and Miles are now squatting."

"Squatting?" He whistled low. "Wow, this just got a lot more complicated."

Josie hesitated, wondering if she'd shared too much. But she couldn't do this alone.

"I still can't believe Miles would agree to something like that. They lived in a rental here before but moved into her house shortly after she passed away."

"But how come Doris seems to be spearheading this blackmail campaign? What's Miles' role in all of this?"

"I'm not sure. I haven't seen or heard from him since the funeral and Doris hasn't mentioned him at all, but he has to be in on this, right?"

He shrugged. "I don't know the guy. What do you think?"

"Miles has always been so sweet—the polar opposite of his wife in just about every way." She looked up at the moon, wishing she knew the answer. "I wish I could talk to him instead of Doris, but my calls to him have gone to voicemail. I was hoping he could help me get my cat back."

"It's getting late," Noah said. "Let's talk this all out tomorrow when our heads are clearer. I can drive you back to your hotel and then pick you up in the morning."

A cool breeze rolled over the hill, making her wish she'd brought a wrap. "Actually, I'd like you to just drop me at my car again."

"One of your tires was slashed, remember? Your car isn't drivable."

"I may not be able to drive it anywhere, but I can sleep in it."

He scowled. "Nothing doing."

"I had only planned to stay one night in Calamity, but this is day four. Besides, the back seat of my car is pretty comfortable, and I can put the money I save toward the tire repair."

He looked at her for a long moment. "Come home with me."

Josie laughed as she slowly shook her head. "Sorry, cowboy, but we're just pretending to be a couple, remember?"

"The way I see it, if you stayed at my place while you're here, that could benefit both of us."

"No—"

He held up his palms. "Just hear me out. You come

back to my ranch house and stay in the guest room. It's even got a lock on the door, so you'll be plenty safe there. And I don't care how comfortable the back seat of your Miata might be, it won't be as cozy as the guest room's king-size bed and attached bath.

Josie was tempted and not just by the thought of a king-size bed. She could get lost in those sexy brown eyes if she wasn't careful. "No strings attached?"

"No strings." He held up two fingers in the Boy Scout salute.

"That sounds tempting," she said, though still wary. He was a stranger, but she'd seen how well liked and respected he was by the people at the wedding. "What's in it for you, Noah?"

"Simple, we continue the ruse that we're in love."

"But I'm going to be leaving for San Antonio as soon as I get my cat back."

He smiled. "That sounds good to me. I always thought a long-distance relationship might be the answer to my problem. At least then, folks around here will finally start minding their own business."

"But it wouldn't be real."

"Of course not. It would just give me time to let everything blow over. Then I'll break up with you."

"Smart," she said, laughing. "It just might work."

"Then it's a deal?" He held out one hand.

"Deal." She reached out to shake it, the warmth of

his touch sending an odd tingle through her. "Starting tomorrow, I'm going to take drastic action. I'm not letting Doris Dooley push me around anymore."

He frowned. "Are you sure that's smart? Just from overhearing that one phone call, she doesn't exactly seem stable."

"I'll take my chances."

"Okay," he said, "then I'm in."

"You are?" she asked, surprised. "Because this could get ugly, and you've already had to face down one scandal."

A cool, brisk wind came up from the west, catching Josie by surprise. She quickly bent down to pull on her shoes and when she stood up, she noticed that Noah had moved and positioned himself to block most of the wind with his body.

"I promised to help you," he said, "and I keep my word. Now we just need to come up with a plan."

"Oh, I have a plan," she said, slowly looking him up and down. "What I really need is a decoy."

Chapter Five

The next morning, Josie opened her eyes, then sat up in bed in a moment of panic. Sunlight streamed through a window with gauzy white curtains, and she could hear a dog barking in the distance. To her surprise, Josie had slept through the night without stirring.

"Noah's house," she whispered, as the events of yesterday came rushing back to her. Her stolen Baby, the car chase, that kiss with Noah. Part dream, part nightmare.

Last night, she'd taken a chance by coming home with a man she'd just met, but once they'd arrived at his ranch, shortly before midnight, he'd been the perfect gentleman. The house had loomed large in the moonlight, at least two stories high with a wide front porch. Inside, Noah had briefly shown her around the first floor, then taken her up to the guest room and wished her a good night's sleep before disappearing down the long hallway.

Now, snug and cozy under a thick bedspread, Josie relished the warm cocoon of the bed, and she was reluctant to leave it. She'd just started to doze off again when she heard the sound of Noah's voice from outside the house, though she couldn't make out his words.

She climbed out of bed, her bare feet padding over a large blue area rug before stepping onto the hardwood floor near the window. Parting the curtain, she squinted against the morning sunshine lighting the room.

Then she caught sight of Noah outside the barn, wearing a sleeveless white t-shirt with his blue jeans and cowboy boots. He held a five-gallon feed bucket in each hand, the heavy weight of them making muscles bulge in his bare arms and shoulders. A large yellow Labrador romped around him.

Josie smiled at the dog's goofy antics.

She turned away from the window, the idyllic scene outside at odds with the chaos inside of her. She wanted to race over to Loretta's house and rescue Baby from the Dooleys, feeling like she'd already wasted too much time. And she needed to find Loretta's will. Which meant she couldn't let Noah, or his cozy homestead, distract her from the reason she'd come to Calamity.

She walked over to the nightstand to check her phone. There were no more cryptic text messages from Doris. However, there was a short message from an old friend who had just heard about her new job at the museum in San Antonio and wanted to wish her good luck.

"Oh, Brett." She exhaled loudly, sending him a quick thank-you text. "If I told you I was on a ranch in the middle of nowhere with a sexy cowboy who promised to help me rescue my kidnapped cat, you wouldn't believe it."

The loud whinny of a horse sent her hurrying back over to the window. Noah was leading a beautiful bay gelding out of the barn.

Josie cranked the window open and shouted. "Hey, are you going riding?"

He looked up in her direction and waved. "I sure am. Do you want to join me?"

"Yes! Don't leave without me!"

She whirled around and moved straight toward her suitcase, where she grabbed a pair of blue jeans and a matching knit top. Josie had loved horseback riding since was seven years old. There was a horse camp for foster kids every summer and she'd been able to attend every year until she'd aged out.

After quickly combing her hair into neat ponytail, she pulled on a pair of sneakers. She'd never owned cowboy boots, but sneakers had worked well enough for riding before. By the time she made it outside, Noah was saddling a second horse, this one a palomino mare.

"They're both so beautiful," Josie said, slowing her steps so she didn't spook the horses. She reached out to gently stroke the neck of the palomino.

"They're my favorite horses for checking fence lines." He tipped up his black cowboy hat. "Have you ridden before?"

Josie nodded. "Yes, I got a lot of riding experience at horse camp when I was a kid, but that's been a while ago."

She let her gaze roam around the yard. It had been too dark to see much when they'd arrived her last night. The house looked even larger in the daylight and was directly across from the barn. A well-kept lawn separated the two.

The front of Noah's house had neat rows of landscaping blocks sectioning off large plots, but there were few plantings. Just a scattering of daylily plants with bright-yellow blooms and some leafy round mounds of chrysanthemums that hadn't started to bloom yet.

"You have a really nice place here," she said. "So big and roomy."

"Thanks. I try to keep everything neat and tidy but sometimes it can get away from me when it starts to get busy around here."

She laughed.

"This is the perfect horse for you," he said, untying the reins of the palomino from the fencepost and handing them to her. "She's got a great disposition and stays pretty calm."

Josie liked watching Noah work with the horses, especially the way he'd stroke them and talk softly to them. For a big man, he had a gentleness that surprised her. She watched him put some tools in a saddlebag, then they mounted their horses and started down the long driveway.

Josie took a deep breath of the fresh country air as she rode. It was a perfect time for a ride, the morning sun warm on her face and a slight breeze ruffling her hair. Still, it was difficult to let go of her worry about Baby and how she could get her back. The one thing she did know is she wasn't leaving Calamity without her cat.

She glanced over at Noah, who rode slightly ahead of her. He sat tall and straight in the saddle, the muscles in his broad shoulders flexing beneath his chambray shirt as he held the reins. For a moment, it all seemed surreal. She hadn't even known this man twenty-four hours ago, and now she was enjoying a morning horseback ride with him.

"We're going to ride the fence line on the south pasture where my Longhorn cattle are grazing." Noah glanced back at her. "I need to make sure there aren't any gaps in the fence where my cattle might break through."

Josie gently spurred on her horse to pull even with him. "How often do you have to do that?"

"This time of year, I usually check it about once a week. The barbed wire can get too loose if a tree limb falls on it or just from natural wear and tear. And cattle can put pressure on it too, because like people, they think grass always looks greener on the other side of the fence."

She chuckled. "That is true."

They kept chatting about cattle and ranch life until they reached the pasture, where they were greeted by the coos of mourning doves in a grove of cottonwood trees. A few cows and a massive bull looked up and watched them as they neared the fence. The rest of the herd grazed on the dewy pasture grass, apparently undisturbed by their presence.

Noah took the lead, slowly walking his horse along the fence line as he studied the hardiness of fenceposts and wire. Josie let her horse fall in behind him, curious to watch him at work. He stopped a couple of times, usually to tighten up a loose wire by hammering it back on a fencepost with a staple-shaped nail.

It was easy for Josie to forget her troubles the longer they rode. She remembered experiencing that same sense of peace at her summer horse camps. If it was in her budget, she'd get a horse of her own to board near her home.

"So, what's in San Antonio?" Noah asked as they finished their fence inspection and rode back toward the barn. "Are you from there?"

She reached out to smooth her hand over the mare's sleek gold coat. "No, I've never been there before. I'm heading down there because I accepted a job offer as the interim curator at a private museum. They specialize in local area artifacts and history."

"Interim? Does that mean you're hoping to get the permanent position?

"Yes, I'm hoping it works out that way. Although, I'm lucky to even be getting this opportunity. I just graduated with my master's degree in history and only have internship experience in the field."

They turned into the long driveway, the horses instinctively heading toward the barn. "Even if they don't hire me for the position," she said. "I'll get great experience to add to my resume."

"That makes sense. Seems like history might be a

tough field to find a job. What made you interested in it?"

Josie hesitated, not sure how much she wanted to share. "I've just always loved reading stories about the past. Time and places can change, but people seem to be pretty much the same through the centuries. For good or for bad."

"I can see that." He slowed his horse to a stop in front of the bar, then climbed down from the saddle. "I'll finish up here if you want to head back to the house."

Josie reluctantly climbed off the saddle, wishing she could just spend time with the horses instead of dealing with the problems that awaited her. But Baby was counting on her. So, the sooner she solved those problems, the sooner she could leave for San Antonio and start making her own history.

When Noah walked through the back door of his house later that morning, he saw Josie sitting at his kitchen table. She'd showered and changed into a sapphire-blue sweater and a pair of black leggings. Her blond hair was still damp and swept up into a high ponytail.

"I see you made coffee," he said, walking over to the sink to wash his hands.

"I hope you don't mind." She cradled a cup of coffee in her hands. "I always need at least one cup to get me going for the day."

He poured a cup for himself before joining her at the table. "I usually make a full pot every morning, then just keep topping off my cup."

She smiled. "A man after my own heart."

He stared down at his cup, feeling a sudden awkwardness at their situation. It was one thing to fake being a couple in front of other people, but having Josie in his home, looking like she belonged there, was something else altogether. "I can cook us some breakfast as soon as I clean up."

She shook her head. "No, I'm fine. I already found some cereal in a cupboard and helped myself. I hope you don't mind."

"Okay, good." Noah cleared his throat. "By the way, I called a friend of mine and he's going to tow your car to his auto shop and give us the damage report on that tire and rim. He promised to call me by this afternoon."

"That sounds good because we need to talk about my plan to rescue Baby and—"

The doorbell rang, cutting her off. They exchanged glances.

"Are you expecting someone?" she asked.

He shook his head and walked toward the front door. "Not this early."

Familiar voices were gabbing on the porch as he opened the door and Noah stifled a groan. Two of the busiest busybodies in town had decided to pay him a visit.

"Morning, cousin!" Shelby Tanner greeted him and sailed past him into the house.

Taylor Tanner winked at him as she followed her sister over the threshold, carrying a covered wicker basket in each hand. "Hope you don't mind a little company, Noah. It's been a while since we paid you a visit."

"This is a surprise," he said dryly, closing the front door behind them. He loved his cousins, but they also knew how to push his buttons. "What brings you here so early?"

"Early?" Shelby exclaimed, making a beeline for Josie. "It's almost nine o'clock. We've been up for hours."

"We'll just stay for a minute," Taylor promised him before joining her sister at the kitchen table. "Aren't you going to introduce us to your pretty guest?"

Noah cleared his throat, watching Josie's smile widen. "Josie, these are my nosy cousins, Shelby and Taylor, and they've come here to gather intel about our relationship. They lease a great coffee shop in a building I own downtown, but apparently, they don't have anything better to do on a Saturday morning."

Shelby laughed. "Good try, Noah, but you're not going to chase us away with that kind of sass. We weren't able to make it to the wedding last night, so we didn't get a chance to meet your new girlfriend."

Josie stood up and held out her hand. "I'm Josie Lou Reid, and I can't wait to see what you have in those baskets."

Taylor chuckled as she shook her hand. "Josie Lou, you're a girl after my own heart. And just ignore Noah's grumpiness. He's not a morning person."

"That's not true. I've been up since dawn and taking care of this ranch, while you two have been plotting to descend on unsuspecting family members." Noah moved closer to the table and peered into one of the baskets. "Of course, I might be more understanding about this unannounced visit if you've got something good in there."

"Get your nose out of that basket, Noah Tanner," Shelby scolded him as he tried to snatch it from her. "You're going to make Josie think you don't love us with that kind of talk. So just admit that we're your favorite cousins and I'll let you have your fill of raspberry muffins, still warm from the oven of Blue Moon Coffee Shop."

"You two are my favorite by a mile," he said, taking a seat at the table. "Josie, just wait until you taste these muffins."

He pulled a raspberry muffin out of the basket, noting the odd expression on her face as she looked between the three of them. "Here you go," he said, setting the wrapped muffin in front of her. He lowered his voice. "Are you okay?"

"Yes," she whispered back. "I'm just enjoying the moment."

The moment stretched into half an hour, with Shelby and Taylor doing most of the talking. Finally, after inhaling four muffins, Noah turned to his cousins. "I'm glad you two could stop by, but we've got some important errands to run this morning."

"Oh my," Shelby said, exchanging a pointed glance with her sister. "That sounds intriguing. Care to share?"

"Nope," he said, rising from the table.

Josie stood up too. "Thank you so much for dropping in. It was a pleasure to meet both of you."

"Oh, honey, the pleasure was all ours," Taylor said. "Now don't let Noah run you off; he can be a little grumpy sometimes."

"He's like a slice of pecan pie," Shelby added. "Crunchy on the outside, but sweet and gooey on the inside."

Noah shook his head. "That's the worst comparison I've ever heard. I'm not a pecan pie."

"You're right." Taylor grinned. "He's more like a peanut roll. Nutty and a little salty."

"Or maybe a honey bun?" Josie chimed in with a mischievous gleam in her eye. "Sweet and irresistible."

"Oh, girl, you've got it bad," Taylor said, and both cousins laughed on their way to the front door.

At the threshold, Shelby turned back. "But all joking aside, Josie. You couldn't find a better cowboy than Noah. He really is a keeper."

Noah felt heat creep up his neck. "Okay, well, thanks for stopping by."

"We do have a small favor to ask of you, Noah," Shelby said.

"Uh-oh." Noah looked between his two cousins. "So those muffins were a bribe?"

Taylor grinned. "I wouldn't put it like that, but some might. Really, though, it's a very small favor. Shelby and I just received a last-minute invitation to a conference for small business owners in Dallas. It starts on Monday, and we just need you to keep an eye on the coffee shop for us while we're gone."

"And maybe open it a couple mornings this week," Shelby added, "when Kayla, our assistant manager, isn't available. You've done it before, so you know it's not hard."

"We'll owe you for this favor, too," Taylor said. "For instance, we'd be happy to watch the ranch if you and Josie decide you want to take off on a romantic getaway somewhere."

"Maybe Hawaii." Shelby wriggled her eyebrows. "Or somewhere in the Caribbean."

Noah held up both hands. "All right, stop trying to convince me. I'll do it."

They both reached out to give him a hug, then kept thanking him as they made their way off the porch. He watched his cousins until they drove away, then he closed the door and turned around to face Josie. "Well, I think we fooled them."

"Did we?" Josie asked, wiping the crumbs off the table. She looked up at Noah. "Is your family always like that?"

"Like what?"

"Just dropping in to see you, cracking jokes, and asking for favors. Like they belong here."

He didn't understand her question, then remembered she grew up in foster care. "I guess so. It's just always been that way, even if they are a little too curious about my love life. At least they're not trying to play matchmaker anymore." He shuddered. "They were exceedingly bad at it."

Josie carried the plates and coffee cups over to the

kitchen sink. “Do you think they’ll be disappointed when I suddenly leave town and never come back?”

He sighed. “I’ll worry about that later. Now, tell me about this rescue plan of yours.”

“First, you need to get cleaned up and ready to go. I’ll fill you in on the way there.”

Chapter Six

Noah cruised his pickup along one of the tree-lined streets in the designated historic district of Calamity. The late-morning sunlight cast a tranquil glow over the stately Tudor, colorful Victorian, and grand colonial homes in the well-kept neighborhood. Somewhere, a dog barked, followed by the sound of children laughing.

"There's Loretta's house." Josie pointed to a Queen Anne Victorian that stood three stories high at the end of the block. "I recognize it from her pictures."

Noah swallowed a groan. He'd already threatened to turn around and take them back to his ranch when he'd heard Josie's plan, but she'd just find a way to come back here without him. That didn't mean he still couldn't try to talk her out of it.

"I meant what I said before, Josie." He eased his

pickup closer to the disaster he was certain awaited them. "Your plan is illogical."

"It's perfect." She pulled her ponytail tighter, then took a deep breath. "And it's the only way I know how to get my cat back and look for Loretta's will."

"You can't just sneak into the house. What if Doris catches you?"

She smiled. "Doris won't catch me because you'll be here to distract her."

"If she even lets me in the door."

"I think you're seriously underestimating your powers of persuasion."

"Huh?"

Her gaze moved over him in a way that made him momentarily forget what they were talking about, and he didn't like that one bit. If he wasn't careful, he'd find himself sitting outside a wedding chapel covered in hives again. After he'd shed his wedding attire last night, the itchy, red welts had almost completely faded away. The message seemed all too clear: Stay single or suffer.

"Besides," Josie said, "I doubt Doris will even be there. She's a security guard at the hospital and works most of the weekend and evening shifts."

"What if she's off today?"

"All you have to do is keep her occupied for about

fifteen minutes. I'll look for Baby first, and then the will."

"And if you don't find either?"

She shook her head. "That's not an option."

He rubbed one hand over his jaw, still not convinced. "There's got to be a better way. What if she thinks you're an intruder and decides to shoot first and ask questions later? If she's a security guard, I assume she owns a gun."

"At last count, she owns five pistols, four semi-automatic handguns, and a twelve-gauge shotgun. Miles told me about them. He's not a fan of guns," Josie said.

"Sounds like he should be even more afraid of his wife."

"That might be why I haven't seen him around. Maybe he's hoping she'll forget about him or find another man to take his place." Josie smiled. "That's where you come in."

"I think I should warn you that I'm not good at pretending. She'll be able to tell I'm faking it from a mile off."

She studied him for a long moment. "I know you can do it. We pulled it off at the reception, didn't we? The word spread so fast that your cousins wanted to check me out this morning and make sure I was good enough for you." She tilted her head. "And you sure didn't seem to have a problem pretending when we kissed last night."

"That was different." He cleared his throat. What was it about this woman that made him want to kiss her again?

Josie smiled at him, then popped open the truck door. "See you in fifteen minutes."

Before he could say another word, she was gone. So much for trying to talk her out of this crazy scheme. He watched as she disappeared behind a tall hedge of evergreen bushes just a few houses away from Loretta's childhood home.

"Damn," he muttered, then shifted into gear.

He slowly glided his pickup along the curb until he reached 401 Chinaberry Street. The house was painted in pleasing hues of yellow, green, and blue. An octagonal tower with stained glass windows stood out in one corner among the steeply pitched roofs. Both the large wraparound porch and the narrow driveway were empty. So was the carport. He couldn't see any signs of life inside or outside the house. Noah sank back against the driver's seat and checked his watch.

Fourteen minutes to go.

He tapped his fingers on the steering wheel, wondering how exactly he'd gotten into this situation. At least Josie wasn't planning to stay in Calamity long. She'd made it clear more than once that she'd be off to

San Antonio as soon as she could. But the longer he sat there, the more he wondered if that actually might be a problem.

He obviously wasn't great at reading women. What if he'd read her all wrong? She loved her cat–of that he was certain. But what about the rest? This business about Loretta's will sounded strange. So did the mysterious Miles. And now Noah was involved in a possible crime. What if Josie took off and left him behind to take the fall for it?

He sat up straight in the driver's seat, his body tensing. There was no reason to think the worst, but he'd better develop a plan of his own to keep her at arm's length. Because he couldn't deny the attraction between them. Or the way her bewitching blue eyes mesmerized him. They changed color with her emotions. Sadness turned them ocean blue. Anger made them deepen to sapphire. And when she laughed, they shimmered with flecks of silver.

He wondered what color emerged with passion.

The loud honk of a car horn jerked him from his reverie. He looked in his rearview mirror and saw a familiar black pickup truck looming up behind him. Noah inwardly cringed when he saw the woman sitting behind the steering wheel.

It was time to sweep Dangerous Doris off her feet.

* * *

Josie climbed over the chain-link fence separating Loretta's backyard from its neighbors. Carefully looking around, she crept up the wide porch steps that led to the back door and peeked inside. The Neighborhood Crime Watch decal on the glass panel wasn't the only thing blocking her view. The closed window blinds prevented her from seeing anything else. She pressed her ear against the cool glass and listened.

Silence.

Maybe Doris really was at work. Or sleeping. Or down in the basement destroying all the genealogy charts and maps that Miles had made. He'd told Josie all about them during his trips to Austin when Loretta was sick.

There was only one way to find out.

She pulled a paper clip from her pocket, bent it open, then slipped one end into the keyhole. It was a trick she'd learned from the older kids at the youth center, where she'd been sent after they couldn't find a foster care placement for her when she was fourteen. She'd learned more about how to survive life in that center than she'd ever learned at school.

The sound of a car horn made her jump, and she paused for a moment, just listening. Josie gave the paper clip a couple of deft twists, hoping she hadn't lost her touch. At last, the latch gave way, and she breathed a sigh of relief. Inching the door open, she winced as it emitted a loud creak. She strained her ears for the slightest indication of someone moving around inside the house. After a long silence, she opened the door just far enough to get a good look inside.

Her breath caught in her throat when she saw the scrolled woodwork moldings and trim adorning the kitchen. It looked original, as did the antique pinewood buffet. The rest of the kitchen décor had seen its glory days in the early 1970s, when the avocado and harvest-gold color scheme reigned.

An old Kelvinator refrigerator hummed in one corner and a cookbook lay open on the small Formica-topped table. The faucet dripped into the stained enamel sink with a steady *tap... tap... tap*. The kitchen was small, but surprisingly cozy. Best of all, it was empty.

With her heart pounding in her chest, Josie stepped inside, closing the back door soundlessly behind her. She tiptoed across the faded yellow linoleum to the arched open doorway that separated the kitchen from the rest of the house. She could now glimpse the large sitting room with its original woodwork and crystal chandelier, the design so exquisite it made her breath catch in her throat. She loved history, and stepping into this house made her feel as if she'd stepped into another century.

Gathering herself, she took a deep, calming breath, remembering her reason for coming here.

The sitting room was dark and empty, all the drapes closed over the windows and a layer of dust on every surface. She stood in the middle of the room, her ears perked for sounds from upper floors, but there was only silence. Josie's tense muscles relaxed a bit, and she was fairly certain now that she was alone. Maybe this wouldn't be so bad, after all. With Doris gone, she could make a thorough search of the place.

She thought briefly about Noah, secure in the knowledge that he was keeping watch from his pickup. Which meant he'd be ready and waiting when she sprung Baby from captivity. So much the better. Having him around was too distracting.

Checking her watch, Josie realized she'd already used four minutes. One thing was for certain. She wasn't leaving without her cat.

Noah pasted a smile on his face and leaned his elbow out the open driver's side window as Doris Dooley walked up to his pickup. Walked might not be the right word for it. Her stride reminded him of a

Sherman tank—ruthless and deliberate, able to mow down anything in her path. Which at the moment was him.

"You're blocking my driveway," Doris announced when she reached his window. "Move it. Now." She spun on her heel and walked away.

"No problem," he said, rolling his pickup forward. Now that he'd seen the dreaded Doris up close, he was beginning to understand why Miles let her rule the roost.

She was a knockout.

Her shoulder-length raven hair curled softly around a perfect heart-shaped face. She wore little makeup, except for the mascara on the thick, black lashes framing her green eyes. Her navy-blue security uniform ran small and did little to conceal her hourglass figure.

Where the hell was Josie?

Ignoring the overwhelming urge to floor the gas pedal and make his escape, he shifted the pickup into Park, then cut the engine. Doris had pulled her pickup truck into the driveway and was heading for the front door by the time he reached her.

"Mrs. Dooley?"

"No soliciting," she snapped, pointing to the sign in the window. The one next to the Armed & Dangerous sticker.

He checked his watch. Still eleven minutes to go. Cursing softly under his breath, he quickly closed the distance between them. "Your husband asked me to stop by when I had some spare time in my schedule."

She turned sharply. "Miles? You've seen Miles?"

He cleared his throat, improvising. "No, but I did speak with him on the phone a couple weeks ago about purchasing some insurance for this house."

She looked him up and down. "You look more like a cowboy than a salesman."

"Selling insurance is a side business for me," he said, certain she wasn't buying it. "There are several home policies that I believe might interest you and your husband."

She unlocked the front door, then turned to him. "Do you provide coverage for missing husbands?"

He hesitated, aware that one misstep could put Josie in danger. "No, but I have several other options that might interest you."

She laughed, then gave him a slow once-over. "I think you just might at that. Come in, Mr.... I'm sorry, I didn't catch your name."

"Calhoun," he said, plucking a name out of the air as he followed her into the house. "Wade Calhoun. But you can just call me Wade."

"Okay, Wade. Have a seat."

Noah looked from the boxy safe-green sofa to the

matching armchair, both at least thirty years old. He chose the armchair, hoping he wouldn't be there long. Hoping even more that Josie wouldn't make a sudden, unexpected appearance.

"Nice place," he said loudly to warn her of their presence.

"Miles inherited the house from his great-aunt. As you can see, she had a real flair for decorating." Doris flipped her keys on top of a large antique sideboard. "Care for a beer?"

Noah held up one hand. "No, thanks. I don't drink on the job."

Doris laughed as she walked into the kitchen. She returned a moment later with two beer cans in her hand, then tossed him one. "Life isn't any fun unless you break some rules."

He caught it one-handed, then popped open the tab. Foam fizzed up through the opening and he took a quick swallow. "Thank you, Mrs. Dooley."

"Call me Doris. I don't consider myself a *Mrs.* anymore." She plopped down on the recliner and rested one foot on top of the walnut coffee table. "My husband took off a week and a half ago."

He sat down on the sofa and decided to play dumb. "I'm sorry. This must be a tough time for you."

She drank long and deep, then wiped the back of her hand across her mouth. "Difficult, hell. It's been driving me crazy. If I ever get my hands on that floozy who stole him from me…" Her grip tightened on her beer can until the aluminum collapsed under the pressure.

"You're probably better off without him," he said, trying to distract her from her lethal fantasies.

She fingered a raven curl behind her ear, as if suddenly self-conscious. "Do you really think so, Wade?"

Uh-oh. He'd seen that expression before. He'd wanted to distract the woman, not encourage her. Now for some fancy footwork. "Of course, it will take you some time to get over him. Time to heal and analyze what went wrong with the relationship."

"I already know what went wrong," she said. "I married a worm. Now I want a man. A real man who knows how to love a woman."

He glanced at his watch, then rose hastily to his feet. Josie's fifteen minutes were almost up. "Well, I won't keep you any longer. I'm sure you're busy."

She frowned. "But you just got here."

He moved toward the door. "I'm not one of those pushy insurance guys who overstays his welcome. They're the ones who give the rest of us a bad name."

"But you haven't even explained any of your policies yet." She set her beer can on the coffee table and got up. "And I realize now that I do have something valuable that needs insurance."

He looked longingly toward the front door. "You might want a few days to think it over. So many folks are overly insured these days."

Her eyes narrowed. "What kind of cowboy salesman are you?"

A lousy one, obviously. He'd much rather work with horses than people. This debacle was also the reason he loved to work alone. Why had he ever offered to come along with Josie in the first place?

But he knew the answer to that question. It was because he'd been brought up to help people. And because he felt guilty for losing her cat in the car chase. And because he'd never met a woman like Josie before.

"Wade?"

He blinked, then looked at Doris. She stood directly in front of him now, her hands braced on her hips and suspicion thinning her red lips. He'd never been less attracted to a woman.

"I'll ask you again," she said, her voice low and whispery. "What kind of salesman are you?"

He flashed a smile. "Okay, I'll confess. This is the first sales call I've ever made. I guess I need to work on my technique a little."

"I'd say more than a little."

He nodded. "You're absolutely right. I'll go home right now and study the manual."

"Not so fast." She grasped his elbow and took a step closer to him. "First, I want to show you something."

Her grip was surprisingly strong. He tried to ease out of it, but she wouldn't let go. "What?"

She flashed him a coquettish smile that made his blood run cold. "Come with me. I think you'll like what you see."

He had to get out of here. *Now.* He'd agreed to be a decoy, not a sex toy. Despite his plan to stay single, Noah wasn't ready to fall into bed with any woman who came along. And he definitely drew the line at married women. Especially married women who owned guns.

But Doris didn't give him a chance to escape. She practically dragged him down the hallway to the last door on the left.

"Here we are."

"Listen, Doris, it's against company policy for salesmen to... fraternize with clients."

"I like to break rules, remember?" She winked at him, then pulled a small key out of her pocket and unlocked the door.

He just hoped she didn't like breaking anything else. Specifically, the bones of men who refused to sleep with her. Not that she'd asked him yet, but a man makes certain assumptions when a woman drags him to her bedroom.

Only it wasn't a bedroom.

He blinked as the door swung open, wondering if he was seeing things. He looked at the beer in his hand, then back at the room.

"This is my hobby room," she announced proudly. "Like it?"

He followed her slowly through the door, taking it all in. The yellow-and-white gingham coverlet and pillows adorning the daybed. The matching window drapes. The plastic ivy plant hanging in the corner. And last, but certainly not least, the wide array of weapons showcased in a long display cabinet on the wall. Brass knuckles. Nunchakus. Stun guns. A veritable buffet of violence.

"What's all this?" he asked, unnerved by the combination of gingham and guns. He became even more unnerved when he glimpsed the pink pedicured toes sticking out from under the floor-length drapes.

Josie.

Her fifteen minutes were now up. So, what the hell was she still doing here? And what would Doris do if she found her?

"This is my collection," she said, pointing in Josie's direction. "Like it?"

Noah would have called it an arsenal, but why quibble? Some people collected stamps; others collected coins. Doris simply had a hobby that was a little different. Then he remembered that she liked to break the rules.

Time to make a quick getaway.

"I could really use another beer, Doris." He gently clasped her elbow, turning her away from the window before she could discover Josie's hiding place. "Why don't we go back in the living room so we can discuss which policy might be the right one for you."

"Not so fast." She kicked the door shut with one foot. "I've saved the best for last." She nodded toward the daybed. "Have a seat."

He clenched his jaw in frustration as he sat down. She unlocked the glass panel on the display cabinet, then reverently removed an old wooden gun case. "These are my pride and joy. Authentic dueling pistols from the nineteenth century. Believe it or not, they're still in perfect working condition."

"That definitely increases their value. Maybe we should take them out into the living room so I can have more light to examine them."

"I'll just open the drapes," she said, moving toward the window.

"No!" He jumped up and took the gun case out of

her hands. "That won't be necessary. Let's have a look at them."

They both sat on the daybed, the springs creaking with their combined weight. He breathed a silent sigh of relief that Doris kept her distance. She waited expectantly as he lifted the lid of the gun case.

He removed the top cloth, instantly met with the combined odors of cleaning fluid and gun oil.

"Well?" she asked at last.

He whistled low as he inspected the dueling pistols. They were in mint condition, well-oiled and ready for action. No doubt they were worth a fortune.

Doris carefully picked one up, caressing the long barrel with one sharp pink fingernail. "Aren't they gorgeous?"

He shifted slightly to block her view of the drapes. "Impressive."

She breathed lightly on the barrel, then rubbed the spot with her sleeve. "The legend is that they belonged to a family from South Texas. The eldest daughter of the family shot and killed a swindler who charmed his way into their home and then tried to steal from them."

She looked up at him. "Isn't it funny how history repeats itself?"

"Uh... I'm not sure what you mean." Noah edged back on the daybed. "By the way, is that thing loaded?"

She smiled, revealing a row of large white capped teeth. "Since I'm the one holding the gun, I'll ask the questions. Let's start with what you're really doing here."

So much for his first, not to mention last, acting stint. "I already told you. I have a side job selling insurance. Your husband—"

"My husband has never paid one red cent for any kind of insurance. Miles doesn't believe in it. Besides, any extra money we had always went into his inventions."

Noah stood up. "Then I should quit wasting your time."

Doris cocked the pistol and pointed it straight at his chest. "Don't leave yet. Maybe you have something else I might be interested in."

Just the words he didn't want to hear. He stared down the wide barrel of the antique pistol, considering his options. "Something else?"

"That's right." She smiled as she rose slowly to her feet. "Take off your clothes."

Chapter Seven

Josie's heart skipped a beat at Doris' words. She stood frozen behind the drapes, afraid to move, afraid not to move. Noah had been right. This was a stupid plan.

"I think I'll leave my clothes on," he said, sounding remarkably calm considering the request. "It's a little chilly in here."

Doris snorted. "It's the middle of September in Texas and I don't have the air-conditioning on."

"I'm cold-blooded."

"Cut the excuses. Take off your clothes so we can get down to business."

Josie heard the sound of Noah clearing his throat. "Exactly what kind of business?"

"I want information."

"I have trouble thinking clearly when I'm naked."

"Yeah, you and every other man on the planet.

Now tell me something I don't know—like the real reason you're in my house. But first, take off your pants."

Josie closed her eyes, trying to think of some way out of this mess. If only she hadn't dragged Noah into it. She'd been desperate at the time, but never imagined Doris would take it this far.

"Listen, Doris—"

"I've had enough of your stalling tactics," Doris said. "If you don't start stripping by the time, I count to three, I'm gonna start shooting. One. Two..."

Josie heard the whir of a zipper, then a few seconds later, the muffled sound of clothes hitting the floor. She didn't want to imagine what was on the other side of those drapes. Well, actually she did, but this was hardly the time or the place.

"That's far enough," Doris ordered. "I'll let you leave your boxer shorts on."

"Gee, thanks," he said dryly.

"You're welcome. Speaking of boxer shorts, I see you're a Mickey Mouse fan."

"Gift from an old girlfriend."

Doris chuckled. "I hope that wasn't a subliminal comment on the size of your... sexual prowess."

"Can we get on with it?" he snapped. "What exactly do you want to know?" Noah didn't sound calm anymore. In fact, if Josie was any judge of temperament, he sounded like he was ready to wring someone's neck. Most likely hers.

"Why don't we start with your name?"

"I already told you my name is Wade Calhoun."

"I remember that you flashed that business card so fast the name on it was a blur. I'm sure you won't mind if I take a little look-see for myself. Now, you just stand nice and still. This pistol has a hair trigger. Any sudden movements and I won't be responsible for my actions."

Josie could hear the rustle of clothes and got a sinking feeling in the pit of her stomach. As if making him strip wasn't enough, Doris was now obviously rifling through the pockets of his shirt and pants.

"Nice billfold," Doris said. "Ah, and here's a driver's license. Nice picture, too. It says right here your name is Noah Tanner."

Josie winced. *Busted.* Her heart raced. She worried what Doris might do with that gun now that she knew he was here under false pretenses.

"I've never cared much for my real name," he said, still valiantly trying to salvage the situation. "Don't you think Calhoun has more pizazz?"

"Well, well, well," Doris said. "And here's a business card: Noah Tanner. Owner and Operator of Triple Creek Ranch." She looked up at him. "No wonder you were such a lousy insurance salesman."

"I told you I'm trying to branch out."

"Spare me, Tanner. Lies make me trigger-happy."

Josie had never felt so helpless in her life. But what could she do? Revealing herself would only make Doris more furious. On the other hand, she couldn't just cower behind the curtains while Noah fought her battle. She squeezed her eyelids shut. *Think, Josie, think.*

"Relax, Doris. You're overreacting."

"And you're hiding something. Or is it someone?"

A cold chill ran over Josie's body. She held her breath and pressed her spine against the windowpane.

"I don't know what you mean," he said.

"I think you do. I think you're the fella who followed me out of that wedding chapel parking lot. And I think this charade was an attempt to distract me. In fact, I'll bet my collection of hand grenades that Josie Reid is searching this house as we speak."

Relief washed over her. So, Doris *hadn't* figured out where she was hiding. Yet.

"Josie who?"

"Don't play dumb, Noah. That woman somehow got you roped into this. I knew she was after my husband for that inheritance. But frankly, now that I've seen you in the flesh, it's clear why she chose you. You're all beefcake, no brains." She shook her head, her gaze raking over him. "Such a waste."

"Can I have my clothes back now?" he snapped.

"I think I'll keep them while I search the rest of the house for that man-eating thief."

"What about me?"

"Well, I've got your clothes, your wallet, and the keys to your pickup truck. So, unless you feel like streaking through this nice neighborhood, you can stay right here. And if you do try to run, I should warn you that I've got some very uptight neighbors. You won't get two blocks before the cops pick you up for indecent exposure."

A scant moment later, Josie heard the sound of the door opening, then closing, shortly followed by the turn of a key in the lock. She slowly released her pent-up breath. Noah was safe.

He was also a little upset.

A lean tanned hand ripped open the drapes and Noah Tanner stood before her. An almost naked Noah Tanner. Her mouth actually went dry at the sight of him. If he ever got tired of the insurance business, he could have a long, lucrative career as a male stripper.

She swallowed hard and tried not to stare. "Nice boxer shorts."

"They were a present. Mickey Mouse has nothing to do with my... sexual prowess. My prowess is just fine, thank you very much. In fact, it's more than fine."

She held up both hands. “Hey, I believe you. Now keep your voice down so Doris doesn’t hear you.”

“Doris isn’t the problem.” He stabbed his index finger toward her. “*You’re* the problem. Ever since I met you, my life has been turned upside down.”

She frowned. “We only met yesterday.”

“Really? Because it seems a lot longer than that. More like an eternity.”

His words only made her feel guiltier. “Look, I know this is all my fault.”

“Damn straight.”

“And I promise to make it up to you.”

He looked skeptical. “How?”

Good question. “Well, the first thing I’ll do is get us out of here.”

“And take the chance of meeting Doris and her prized pistol outside that door? No, thank you.”

“We’ll go out the window.” She looked at Noah again, distracted by all that bare skin. Not to mention the muscles rippling across his taut stomach.

For the first time, the full impact of their fake romance really hit her. Because if it was real, then she’d be touching that body. Caressing those broad shoulders. Breathing in the scent of his skin. Kissing that firm, truculent mouth.

Her knees turned to jelly at the thought. She took a deep breath, pushing the images from her mind.

Now was not the time to get pulled into a sexual fantasy. Even if that fantasy was standing right in front of her.

She turned to the daybed, removing the quilted coverlet on top, then stripped off the yellow gingham sheet underneath.

"Here," she said, wrapping it around him toga style. "This will help."

"You're right," he said wryly. "This is so much better. I'm sure no one will even give me a second glance."

"It's this or Mickey Mouse. Take your pick."

"Fine," he bit out. "If we come across a toga party, I'll be ready."

She grinned. "I love a man who looks on the bright side."

Panic flared in his blue eyes. "What do you mean by love?"

She shook her head as she turned to the window. "Keep your shorts on, Tanner. It's just a figure of speech. I know how skittish you are about love and marriage."

"Skittish? Try allergic."

"Believe me, I know." She turned to crank open the window. "For what it's worth, I *am* sorry for getting you into this mess."

"I just want to get out of here."

Josie popped out the screen. "Grab that chair over there."

Noah held up his sheet with one hand as he pulled the wooden desk chair into position under the window. "Ladies first."

She flashed a smile at him as she stepped up onto the chair. "Thank you."

"Don't mention it. But if Doris starts shooting, you're on your own."

So much for chivalry. Josie swung one leg out the window, then jumped into the marigold bed on the other side. "At least we're on the ground level."

"Are you always this optimistic?" he asked after following her out the window.

"Yes."

"I really hate that." He adjusted his gingham toga, then glanced toward the closed front door.

"Ready to make a run for it?"

"Where exactly are we running to?"

"Your pickup. On the count of three. One, two..." Josie took off, hearing Noah's muttered oaths behind her. She sprinted for his blue pickup, her heart pounding in her chest, knowing that any moment Doris could see them and open fire. At last, she reached the passenger door, yanked it open, then dove inside, scrambling into the driver's seat to make room for Noah.

A split second later, Noah jumped in behind her. "We were supposed to go on three."

Josie struggled to catch her breath. "Yeah, but your legs are longer. I was afraid you'd get here first and leave without me."

He stared at her. "That would be hard to do since I don't have any keys. But more importantly, do you think I'd actually leave you here at the mercy of Doris?"

"Doris has no mercy, or didn't you notice?"

"I noticed. She does have a nice gun collection though." He adjusted the sheet over his hips. "But I still can't believe you think I'd leave you behind. Didn't I miss my best friend's wedding to go after your cat?"

"You thought it was a baby."

"Which proves my point. Babies make me nervous, yet I didn't even hesitate."

She bent under the steering wheel and pulled several different-colored wires out from underneath the dash and began splicing two wires together.

"What do you think you're doing?"

She didn't say anything for a moment, her concentration focused on the wires in her hand. "I'm hot-wiring your truck. Doris has your keys, remember?"

"Hot-wiring my truck?" he echoed. "Where in the world did you learn to do that?"

"It's a long story." She'd learned to keep that part of her past a secret since it seemed to upset people, and Noah was upset enough already.

"I'm very impressed," he said after the engine turned over. "Now, let's get out of here!"

She shifted into drive, then peeled away from the curb. "Do you think Doris saw us?"

He glanced out the back window. "No. Her pickup truck is still parked in the driveway. But it won't take her too long to figure it out."

"Then what?"

"Then Dangerous Doris comes after us." He raked one hand through his hair. "She has my clothes, my wallet, and my keys—including the key to my house. She also has my driver's license and business card, which means she knows where to find me. And since she suspects I'm involved with you, I have no doubt she'll be paying us a visit."

"Do you really believe she's dangerous?"

"I believed it enough to take off my clothes."

Josie's hands flexed on the steering wheel. "Well, if you want some good news, I found Baby."

He turned to her. "You did?"

She nodded. "I was in the basement and heard her in the small space between the floor foundation on the south side of the house. There's plenty of room for a cat, but no human can crawl under there, especially since most of the room is stuffed full of antiques and books and boxes. Her cat carrier is down there also, but it was standing empty. My guess is she got away from Doris when she tried to take her out of the carrier."

"And now Doris can't catch her down there." Noah nodded. "Well, that's a relief."

"Yes," she agreed. "My plan was to see if she would come to me after I found Loretta's will. But I never had the chance. Fortunately, there was a big bag of cat food down there and I filled up a big bowl with water and placed it in that narrow space, so she'll be all right until I have the chance to come back."

He scowled at her. "You can't go back there. That woman is nuts!"

"I don't have a choice. I still need that will and I'm not leaving Baby there forever. I just need a better plan."

"Don't you mean *we* need a better plan?"

She couldn't believe what he was saying. "No, you've done more than enough. I can handle it from here. At least I know my cat is safe and where to find her."

Noah didn't say anything for a long moment. His next words were very quiet and measured. "You've got two choices, Josie. One, I go to the sheriff and lay it all out. Or two, you let me help, because it sure isn't safe for you to go it alone."

To her dismay, tears pricked her eyes. She blinked them and sucked in a deep breath. He had no idea how long she'd been going it alone. But he'd already lost his clothes and his dignity. She couldn't risk his life, too.

"For some reason, Doris always seems to be one step ahead of me," she explained. "She's the type to hold a grudge, so you should keep out of it. She's probably already filing breaking and entering charges as we speak."

"Speaking of breaking and entering, how did you get into her house? And now that I think of it, that hobby room of hers was locked, too."

She hesitated. "I sort of have this talent with paper clips."

He glanced over at her. "What kind of talent?"

She focused her gaze on the street. "I know how to jimmy locks with a paper clip. I used one to open the back door to her kitchen and also to open that hobby room of hers. I figured there was a good chance Baby might be behind a locked door."

"And you must have heard us coming and hid behind the drapes."

She nodded. "That's why I don't want you involved anymore. You've already done more than enough."

He shook his head. "I'm involved now whether I like it or not. Doris isn't going to give up, and I don't have that many clothes." He glanced down at the bedsheet. "Let's head back to the ranch so I can get dressed. I should also put a hold on my bank account since Doris now has my debit card."

She pulled up to the stoplight. "Then what?"

He sighed. "Good question."

Noah watched Josie kneel outside the front door of his ranch house, twisting one end of a paper clip into the keyhole. Her tongue touched the corner of her mouth and her brow furrowed in concentration.

He stood behind her, wrapped in the yellow gingham sheet. He couldn't help but notice the way her blond hair, swept back in a ponytail, curled at the ends. She seemed unfazed by what had happened in that house. He still couldn't quite believe what had happened—and how easily they'd been able to escape.

A click sounded and she smiled up at him. "We're in."

Noah glanced at his watch. "Twenty seconds. It only took you twenty seconds to break into my house."

"You're the one who didn't want to ask your granny for your extra key."

"Can you imagine what would happen if I showed up at her door like this? I'd never hear the end of it from her or the rest of my family." He closed the door behind him and locked it. "I'd rather walk barefoot through a field of sandburs than let Shelby and Taylor find out what happened to me."

He turned to see Josie staring at him and his body tightened at her perusal. A normal reaction to having a beautiful woman in his home, he told himself. If it were any other woman, right about now, he'd be opening a bottle of wine, setting up the record player with his favorite country album, and finding a much better use for this sheet.

Her gaze rose to meet his and something stirred deep inside of him. Her blue eyes didn't waver; she just looked into him as if she could see through to his soul. Almost without thought, he took a step closer to her. Then another.

She stood watching him, waiting, the air between them crackling with expectation. Fortunately, his common sense kicked in before it was too late, bringing him to a halt.

This wasn't just any beautiful woman. This was Josie. The woman who'd hijacked him in a parking lot and picked locks and traveled with a cat.

He'd only met her yesterday, and it was already clear that she was the wrong woman for him. Wrong with a capital *W*. Even if she did have incredible eyes and a body that could keep him up all night.

"Aren't you going to answer it?"

He blinked, then realized his cell phone was ringing. "Oh... yeah, I bet it's the auto shop with an estimate for your tire." He picked it up and clicked on the speaker button. "Hello?"

"Well, hello there, Wade. Or should I say Noah? This is Doris Dooley. I'm sorry you had to leave so quickly because I have an insurance question for you."

Noah's grip tightened on the phone as he glanced over at Josie, but he didn't say a word.

"If I took out a life insurance policy on another person," Doris said, "say for example, a policy on a man who tried to dupe me? Is there a double indemnity clause if he dies in a terrible accident?"

Her husky chuckle carried over the line. "I'm just curious. Stop by anytime. You know where I live. And I know where you live... so I may just stop in for a surprise visit at your ranch one of these days. Bye-bye."

Noah ended the call, shaking his head as he set the phone on the table in front of him.

"I can't believe it!" Josie glared down at his cell phone, her hands curled into fists and her eyes wide. "She just threatened to kill you."

"Not directly, but the message was clear." He shrugged, more amused than anything. "Doris obviously gets a big thrill out of intimidating people. It probably gives her a sense of power, but that doesn't mean she's going to follow through."

Josie began pacing back and forth over the hardwood floor. "But what if she does? What if she has completely lost it?"

He moved toward her, then stopped, reminding himself not to get too close. "Doris knows exactly what she's doing. My bet is she's trying to put more pressure on you to turn over the will."

"The will I couldn't find." She shook her head. "I just hope I get another chance."

"Good thing she doesn't know it's right under her nose." He rubbed his chin, his mind going over her words again. "Doris is desperate, but smart. Did you listen to that message? She knew better than to threaten me outright, so she turned it into a game."

"A game," Josie echoed, her brow crinkled. "You're right. She wants to play games."

The sheet slipped and he tugged it back into place. "I need to change. I'll be right back."

Taking the stairs two at a time, Noah escaped into his bedroom, closing the door behind him. He unwound the sheet from his body. Once he'd donned a pair of Levi's and a blue polo shirt, he didn't feel quite so rattled. Hopefully, he could handle his attraction to Josie better now that he was fully clothed.

The real problem was Doris Dooley.

Despite what he'd told Josie, he knew this game could turn dangerous in a hurry. Doris knew where he lived. She'd already disabled Josie's car and stolen her cat. What would she do next? And could he live with himself if anything happened to Josie? They'd been faking a romance, but there was something about her...

Noah shook himself, not ready to believe he was falling for Josie after just meeting her. And could he even trust those feelings, given his poor track record with women?

That question didn't need an answer. All that mattered was protecting her. So, until this mess was resolved, he couldn't let her out of his sight. And that might be a problem, because the more time he spent with her, the more he wanted her.

Last night, he'd tossed and turned in bed, unable to sleep knowing she was just down the hallway. Even now, closing his eyes, he could imagine her silky blond hair tousled on a pillow and moonlight from the window spilling over the silhouette of her body beneath the bedcovers.

Noah opened his eyes, trying to banish that fantasy from his brain. He had enough problems without adding a romance to the mix. And he needed a clear head to figure out what to do next.

By the time he returned to the living room, he had

an idea. That's where he found Josie pacing back and forth in front of the leather sofa. "Are you okay?"

She looked up at him, worry swimming in her blue eyes. "No. I'm not okay. I've pulled you into this mess and put you in danger. When I think of Doris holding you at gunpoint..." Her eyes closed as she shook her head. "I never should have hijacked your pickup truck yesterday and dragged you into this mess."

Despite the problems she'd caused him, Noah found himself wanting to comfort her. "We can't change the past." He closed the distance between them. "And I'm fine. Doris is a little unhinged, but I guess it could have been worse."

"That's what I'm afraid of—that it will get worse." She looked up at him. "Maybe you should go stay at your granny's house for a few days. Doris won't be able to find you there, so you'll be safe."

"I'm not going anywhere. I've got a ranch to run. And my horses would miss me too much."

"Noah, this isn't a joke."

"I agree. But running away isn't the answer. How would it look if I abandoned you and something bad happened?"

She took a step back from him, her eyes wide. "That's what you're worried about? What people around here will think of you?"

"No, I just..." Noah struggled to find a good explanation for the dumb words that had spilled out of his mouth.

But Josie wasn't interested in his explanation. "I get it, Noah. I'm only here because you want everyone in Calamity to think we're in love. So, if something happens to me, the rumor mill starts up again about Noah Tanner."

He held up both hands. "Hold on, that's not what I meant. It came out wrong."

"Then what did you mean?"

He sucked in a deep breath, meeting her gaze. "I don't run away, Josie. Especially when things get tough. My parents both ran—in their own way. And I swore I'd never be like them. So, what I meant to say is that I'm not leaving your side until I know you're safe."

"Oh," she said, her tone gentler now. "Okay, I understand. I'm sorry for getting worked up. That phone call just proves that Doris isn't going to stop. And the thought of something happening to you because of me..."

"It won't," he promised her. "As your pretend lover, I won't allow that to happen."

She laughed. "Oh, it's lover now?"

"Well, we are living together," he said with a shrug. "People are going to assume."

Josie began to pace again. "That gives me an idea.

Doris assumes I'm trying to steal Miles from her. She seems to be more upset about that than the new will. But what if we prove her wrong?"

"How do we do that?"

She turned to face him. "We find Miles."

Noah nodded, impressed with her brains and beauty—a lethal combination. "If we do find him, do you think she'd agree to a trade? Miles for your cat?"

"Not a trade. I wouldn't put Miles in that position. But it might be the beginning of a negotiation. Even better, Miles might be able to get through to Doris."

"Or at least distract her long enough for us to get in that house again. Then we can find the will and get your cat, leaving Doris without any cards to play."

"Break into the house again?" she said with a smile. "And here I thought you were a wholesome cowboy."

He took a step closer to her. "Not that wholesome."

A blush crept up her cheeks and he could hear the quick intake of her breath.

"That's good to hear," she said. "Because I might need a partner in crime."

He hesitated, doubts beginning to creep in as he thought about her plan. "I don't know. What if it's actually more dangerous to get her hopes up about reuniting with Miles?"

Josie gazed into his eyes. "Don't go soft on me now, Noah. This is the woman who confiscated your clothes."

"I know, but..."

"The woman who held you at gunpoint."

"True, but..."

She took a step closer to him. "The woman who made fun of your Mickey Mouse boxer shorts."

His jaw clenched. "You're right. She has to pay."

The next morning, after her meeting with Mr. Lewiston, Josie walked into Blue Moon Coffee. She was eager to tell Noah what she'd learned from Loretta's attorney. Spying only one empty table, she hurried over to take a seat, pulling back the rustic wooden chair as she inhaled the aroma of fresh-brewed coffee.

A glass display case near the front of the shop was filled with colorful pastries of all shapes and sizes. Her mouth watered when she spotted a large cinnamon roll smothered in silky white frosting.

Her gaze moved to the coffee station, where she saw Noah talking to a middle-aged woman behind the long white quartz countertop. He was dressed like a cowboy, except for the white apron strapped around his waist.

Somehow, it made him look even sexier.

He caught her eye and smiled, then turned his attention to a large espresso machine. Josie watched him, wondering how often he filled in for Shelby and Taylor at their coffee shop because he appeared very comfortable in the role. Or maybe that's just what family did for each other—without expecting anything in return.

Before she could contemplate it any further, Noah walked toward her table carrying two coffee mugs. He set one in front of her. "I brewed up a Tanner family favorite for you. Hope you like it." He sat down in the chair opposite her, his broad tanned hands wrapped around his own large cup.

The steam from the coffee drifted up, warming her cheeks. She could smell cinnamon and chai. She lifted the cup and took a cautious sip. "Mmm," she intoned with an appreciative moan. "That is delicious."

"I aim to please." He grinned as he lifted his own cup. "Now tell me about your meeting with Loretta's lawyer."

She took another sip of her coffee before replying, then set it back on the table. "Mr. Lewiston is a very nice man. And incredibly thorough. After I told him my story about Loretta, he revealed that he'd received a letter from her shortly before her death, explaining the situation. He told me that letter should prevent any successful challenges to the authenticity of her new will."

"Did the letter she wrote to him explain why she changed her will?"

Josie sighed. "No, apparently not. He seemed just as curious to find out what changes she made. I told him I'd bring him the will as soon as I find it."

"Unless Doris finds it first and destroys it."

She shook her head. "I can't let that happen. I made a promise to Loretta, and I intend to keep it. If Miles were here, maybe he could help. Or at least distract Doris long enough for me to conduct a thorough search of that house."

The door to the coffeehouse opened and Josie glanced over to see two grizzled cowboys walk inside. They each had weather-worn wrinkles and gray hair under their cowboy hat. One was shorter than the other and had a slight limp. But they both beamed when they spotted Noah.

"There he is!" the shorter man called out. "Little Noah, back in the old stomping grounds."

Josie bit back a smile as "little" Noah rose to his feet and towered over the two cowboys. "Hey there, Rusty. It's been a long time." He waved to the taller cowboy. "Nice to see you too, Phil."

Rusty walked over and clapped Noah on the shoulder. "Much too long, boy. It's good to see you."

He winked at Josie. “And who’s this pretty young filly?”

She rose to her feet and extended her hand. “Hi, I’m Josie Reid.”

Rusty gave her a firm handshake. “Pleasure to meet you, ma’am.” He looked over at Phil. “Come over here and shake this lady’s hand. We want her to feel welcome here, so she sticks around. There aren’t that many eligible women in Calamity left for Noah.”

Josie reached out to shake Phil’s hand, trying not to laugh at the pained expression on Noah’s face. She was beginning to understand why he’d felt compelled to fake a romance with her. “It’s nice to meet you, Phil. Would you two like to join us?”

“No, thank you, ma’am,” Phil said shyly, removing his cowboy hat. “We’re ordering our coffee to go.” He looked around the shop. “I still can’t believe how much this place has changed.”

“Changed?” Josie echoed.

“It used to be a bar,” Rusty said. “Didn’t Noah tell you about it?”

Noah cleared his throat. “I didn’t want to bore her with too many stories. You know how that drives eligible women away.”

“That is true,” Rusty mused, turning to Josie. “So, I’ll fill you in. Noah’s dad, Huck Tanner, bought this building right after he married Noah’s mom. He fixed it up and turned it into one of the most popular joints in town."

"That's right," Phil said, nodding. "Huck sure did know how to pour a strong whiskey."

"And he could drink any one of us under the table." Rusty sighed. "Those were the days."

"That's exactly the reason," Noah said, cutting into their reverie, "that I decided to close the bar after Dad died, just to give your livers a chance to recover."

Chapter Nine

Josie watched the exchange between the three men with interest. They seemed so comfortable with each other, yet she sensed an undercurrent of tension in Noah. Then again, maybe he had good reason to be tense since Doris had threatened his life. Which made her mission to find Miles even more urgent.

"Hey, we better get going." Phil nudged Rusty with an elbow to the ribs. "We have cattle to move this morning."

"Let's top off our coffee cups and skedaddle." Rusty turned to Josie. "It was very nice to meet you, young lady. I hope you stick around awhile."

"Me too," Phil said, then looked at Noah. "Be smart now, and don't let this one get away."

"You just worry about your own love life." Noah sat back in his chair. "And I'll worry about mine."

"Suit yourself," Phil said with a shrug, then followed Rusty to the front counter.

When they were alone, Noah's mouth curved into a smile. "One thing you can say about those two, they like to talk. And they like you."

"They're entertaining, that's for sure." Josie's gaze followed the two cowboys as they made their way out the door. She glanced at her watch. "How much longer do you have to stay here?"

"I'm done for today. Kayla told me she can handle it from here." Noah took another sip of his coffee. "By the way, the auto shop called and told me your car will be ready tomorrow."

"Finally!" Josie hoped this was a sign that things were starting to move in the right direction. It was strange to think that she could be leaving Calamity soon and would never see Noah again.

"Something on your mind?" he asked, watching her.

She had so many things on her mind it was difficult to keep them all straight. But there was something about sitting at this table with him, talking over a cup of coffee, that seemed oddly intimate, even with the chattering of other patrons around them. "I was thinking about what you said last night."

He shrugged. "Could you be more specific?"

"You said your parents both ran." She gazed into

his brown eyes, hoping she wasn't crossing a line. "What did you mean by that?"

He was silent for a long moment, his gaze not flinching from hers. "I guess it's not a secret around here. You just heard Rusty and Phil reminisce about my dad's bar. He did pour a lot of whiskey—including for himself. He was an alcoholic, but still able to function in public most of the time. In private, he was a mess. That's why my mom left when I was eight."

Josie was stunned. She'd been so focused on her own dysfunctional childhood that she'd never imagined Noah might have ghosts in his past too. "And she didn't take you with her?"

"She tried." Noah rotated the cup in his hands, his expression fixed on the past. "But my dad always made it difficult. Because whenever she did spend time with me, he'd find a way to punish me for it. Not physically," he added quickly. "But in other ways. For instance, I was in junior rodeo and loved it. But he made me quit, saying it would interfere with visiting my mom. Things like that. Until she felt that leaving Calamity—and me—behind was the only way to make my life better."

"I'm sorry," Josie breathed.

He shrugged. "It was a long time ago. And I had my granny and extended family here to take care of me and keep my dad in check. I usually spent more time with all of them than I did at home."

"Do you see your mom now?" Josie asked.

He shook his head. "No, Mom passed away from kidney disease a few months before my dad died of a heart attack. Mom used to send me letters through my granny, so I know she loved me. And that's something my dad could never take away from me."

"I'm sorry that happend to you."

He cleared his throat. "Well, that's enough about me. It's all in the past, but it taught me that marriage can be a disaster. That's why I'm determined to avoid it at all costs."

"But you were going to marry Amber."

"That's right. Shawn and Amber saved me from making the biggest mistake of my life." Noah leaned back in his chair. "What's our plan for today?"

Josie realized he was right. It was better to focus on the future. And her future was in San Antonio. "I think there might be a way to find Miles."

Surprise lit his face. "Let's do it. Where do we go from here?"

"The town morgue."

He blinked. "You think Miles is dead?"

That unsettling possibility had occurred to her, but she knew in her gut that Doris would never hurt her husband. "No, but he used to work there. Maybe one of his former coworkers knows how to reach him."

Noah looked thoughtful. "And if we locate Miles, we can get access to the house again—the legal way this time."

"I hope so because I miss Baby so much." Her throat caught, but she swallowed back a small sob. She needed to stay strong and see this through. "And the sooner I find that new will and deliver it to Loretta's attorney, the sooner I'll be out of your life forever."

* * *

A brief time later, Noah stood with Josie outside the town morgue. It was located on the east side of Calamity, near the industrial district. The red brick building housing the morgue was tucked neatly between a storage facility and a welding business.

He'd almost forgotten this place existed. The fact that Miles Dooley worked at a morgue made him uneasy. Josie paused by the entrance, the sun painting golden streaks in her hair. A tiny locket nestled in the V-neck of her white cotton blouse and a slow smile curved her mouth. She turned to him. "Ready?"

Something shifted inside of Noah. Something... *unusual.* He tried to shake it off as he held the door open for her. He told himself he was probably coming down with the flu as he followed her inside.

"I've got a really good feeling about this," she said to him, her blue eyes gleaming with excitement.

He couldn't help but smile. "You said the same thing about that mental hospital, remember? But we didn't find Miles there, either."

"You're the one who said any man crazy enough to marry Doris belongs in a mental hospital. I was just following through on your hunch."

"Actually, I said any man crazy enough to *marry* belongs in a mental hospital." He followed her up the long flight of concrete steps that led to set of double doors, definitely enjoying the view from behind. But then, he enjoyed viewing Josie Reid from every angle.

Surprisingly, he also enjoyed spending time with her. Before his failed engagement, most of his previous relationships with women had been based on physical attraction. He'd never been interested in much more than a fun fling.

But Josie was different.

She was smart, fun, and unpredictable. Which could be a dangerous combination if she planned to stick around Calamity. But he knew for certain how eager she was to start her new life in San Antonio.

A heavy disinfectant odor permeated the air. He wrinkled his nose. "Maybe I should wait right here."

"Are you chicken?" she teased, taking a step closer to him.

"Of course not." He glanced uneasily down the long sterile hallway. "I just think we should reconsider our strategy. This is a delicate situation."

She laughed. "You *are* chicken." She pointed toward the door. "You can go back and wait outside if this place makes you uncomfortable. I don't mind taking the lead on this."

The only thing making him uncomfortable was how much he wanted to kiss her—while they were standing in a morgue. He forced his attention back on the problem at hand. "The way I see it, we have one shot at this, and we'd better get it right. What do you know about this friend of Miles?"

"Just that his name is Lou Murillo and that they used to hang out together after work." Josie looked thoughtful. "Maybe we should have called him first instead of just showing up."

Noah shook his head. "The best way to get information from people is to catch them off guard. Trust me."

She looked steadily into his eyes. "I do."

Her words should have scared him. The expression on her face should have sent him into a panic. Instead, he experienced a slight inward shift again, like someone trying to find his sea legs on a gently rocking boat.

"Good," he said, trying to keep his focus. "Then I think it's best if *you* wait here."

She frowned. "Why?"

"Because Lou might be more willing to open up to me, you know, man-to-man. He'll be too nervous if you're there." Hell, she made *him* nervous, and he'd been around beautiful women all his adult life.

"Am I that intimidating?"

"That's not exactly the word I'd use to describe you." He reached out one hand to gently brush a stray lock of hair off her temple.

Her blue eyes softened at his touch. "Then what word would you use? As my pretend boyfriend, of course."

"If I tell you, will you wait in the hallway while I interview Lou?"

Her eyes narrowed. "You don't play fair."

"So, what's it going to be?"

She regarded him thoughtfully. "If you really think it's best, I'll wait out here. I'd rather be the one grilling Lou, but all that really matters to me is getting the information about Miles."

He winked at her, then turned down the hallway. "Wish me luck."

"Hey, wait a minute," she called after him. "What's the word?"

Noah turned around, walking backward now so he could see her. "What word?"

She made an impatient gesture with her hands. "The word you'd use to describe me."

"Oh, I made a mistake. There are two words."

"Well?" she said warily.

"I'd say you're... radiant and resilient."

Her mouth hung open, and he grinned as he made a quick escape around the corner. He cleared his throat and sobered his expression, telling himself he shouldn't be this cheerful in a morgue.

He walked down another long, narrow hallway, following the posted signs and acutely aware of the loud echo of his cowboy boots on the concrete floor. Another set of double doors led to a small reception area, where he was met by a cool blast from an air-conditioner vent in the ceiling and an even cooler brunette at the reception desk. She wore a killer red dress with lipstick to match.

Finally, a woman with the right dimensions to take his mind off Josie. Only the longer he looked at her, the more he realized she didn't entice him at all.

A surge of alarm ran through him. Something was wrong. Something was very wrong. He liked cool brunettes. In fact, they'd always been at the top of his list. He took a deep breath and stared into her curious brown eyes. Nothing. Nada. Zilch.

"May I help you?" Her voice was low and throaty.

And it didn't affect him a bit. He took another deep breath, telling himself not to panic. This was a fluke. An aberration. It didn't mean he was falling for Josie. And it certainly didn't mean he'd never find another woman attractive.

She arched one perfect brow. "Sir?"

He cleared his throat, desperately trying to summon up an impromptu fantasy about the brunette seated in front of him. But the only woman in his fantasies had blond hair and blue eyes and an incredibly luscious mouth. This was bad. This was very bad.

"Should I call a doctor?"

"No," he said, collecting himself. A doctor would only make matters worse when he discovered the sultry brunette hadn't raised Noah's pulse even a fraction of a beat. "I'm perfectly fine."

It was a lie. He wasn't fine. If he was fine, he'd be flirting with this woman. Admiring her figure. Paying her compliments and angling for a date. But he didn't have the energy or the desire to do anything of those things.

It was pathetic.

Especially since he'd been intensely aware of Josie since she'd jumped in his pickup truck. The way her hair smelled like vanilla. The way her forehead crinkled whenever she was deep in thought. The way she'd licked the butter off her fingertips when they shared a big bowl of popcorn last night.

Even worse, he'd been dreaming about her. Hot, murky dreams that prominently featured her long legs and her unforgettable face and everything in between.

He tugged at his shirt collar, wondering when the air conditioner had shut off. He looked at the receptionist, not surprised to find her still staring at him. "I'm looking for a man."

She opened the file folder on her desk. "Dead or alive?"

"Preferably alive. His name is Lou Murillo."

She stiffened, then slowly closed the file in front of her and stood up. "Follow me, please."

As he trailed after the woman down another long hallway, his despair deepened. The slow swing of her hips had absolutely no effect on him. He might as well throw his little black book away. Or maybe he should auction it off—earn enough money for a getaway to a tropical paradise where he could forget all about Josie.

The receptionist led him into a small windowless break room. An old refrigerator hummed in one corner, next to a small table littered with candy wrappers. He watched as she stared at the empty wastebasket for a long, silent moment, then turned to face him. "Why do you want to see Lou?"

"It's personal."

She smiled coyly at him. "You can tell me."

He forced a smile, growing impatient. Especially since Josie was cooling her heels in the hallway. "I should introduce myself. I'm Noah. Noah Tanner."

She didn't smile back "Why are you really here, Mr. Tanner?"

"I'm looking for Miles Dooley," he said. "He works here—or used to—with another employee named Lou Murillo. Now, if you stop wasting my time and point me toward Lou—"

"I'm right here," she said. "My name is Louisa Murillo. And Miles is the only person in this town who calls me Lou." Concern filled her eyes as she took a step toward him. "Did he send you here? Is he okay?"

He blinked. "You're Lou?"

She nodded. "Miles and I have been friends for years. In fact, he helped me get this job. But his wife is the jealous type, so he's always referred to me as Lou, so she wouldn't get the wrong idea about me."

"Have you ever met Doris Dooley in person?"

"No, but I've heard she can be scary."

He gave a short nod. "That's one way to describe her. But what is your relationship with Miles. Is it... romantic?"

She started laughing. "Oh my, no! We're just good

friends. Miles loves his wife, despite their problems. He'd just ask me for advice sometimes when things got rocky at home."

"Did that happen a lot?"

She hesitated, giving him the once-over. "Occasionally. The way Miles talks about Doris, she seems pretty strong-minded. And Miles is just the opposite."

"When was the last time you saw him?"

"About three weeks ago."

Noah sank down in an empty chair, trying to figure out what to do next. "How long have you known Miles?"

"Since *Seven Brides for Seven Brothers*," Lou said. "That's a musical that ran at the Calamity playhouse about five years ago. Miles was the prop man and I played one of the brothers."

Noah arched a brow. "You look more like the bride type to me."

"Thanks, but there weren't enough male actors, so a few of us gals had to take those parts. I think we pulled it off pretty well."

"I can imagine," Noah said dryly.

"Miles actually helped me quite a bit. He has a good eye for color and helped me pick out the right wig and clothes and makeup."

"Too bad he has such bad taste in wives."

Lou frowned. "Yeah. It's strange I haven't heard from him. I tried calling him a couple of times, but the calls wouldn't go through. I just thought he'd turned off his phone for some peace and quiet." Worry furrowed her brow. "But I don't believe he'd leave town without telling me."

"Please, think hard. Do you have any idea where Miles might be?"

She chewed her lower lip, then shook her head. "I'm sorry, I don't know. In fact, the more I think about it, the stranger it seems. If he did leave, he sure wouldn't get very far. Miles told me once that Doris controlled all their money. She used to give him an allowance. Just a few bucks a week. Can you believe it?"

Noah pondered that for a moment. "So, there's a good chance he's still in Calamity."

Lou nodded. "I'd say so." She walked over to her desk and pulled a notepad toward her. "I'll give you a list of some of Miles' friends around town—the ones I know, anyway. Maybe they can help."

"I appreciate that." Noah rubbed his jaw, thoroughly frustrated. "If I leave you my phone number, will you give me a call if you hear from him?"

"Sure thing," Lou said, scribbling on the notepad. She tore off the page on the top and handed it to him.

"But if you want my opinion, maybe you shouldn't be looking for Miles." She sucked in a deep, quavering breath. "Maybe you should be looking for Miles' body."

Chapter Ten

Noah wheeled his pickup truck onto the long gravel driveway of Triple Creek Ranch. They'd spent all day tracking down the names on Lou's list and asking questions about Miles. Unfortunately, any leads they'd been given had all come to a dead end. The man hadn't been seen in weeks and no one seemed to know where to find him.

Now he was tired, frustrated, and hungry. It didn't help that they'd picked up a bucket of fried chicken on the way home and the savory aroma kept making his stomach growl.

"That's strange," Josie said, looking out the passenger window. "All the lights are on in your house."

He looked up at the big two-story house, a light

blazing in every window. It was almost dusk, with the sun dropping low behind the barn roof.

"Were you expecting someone?" she asked.

"No, and there aren't any cars parked in front of the house. But it's possible Granny stopped by and dropped off a pie. She has a house key and likes to make sure my refrigerator and pantry are well stocked."

"I think I could eat an entire pie right now." She grabbed the bucket of chicken from the back seat, then climbed out of the pickup. "I don't know about you, but I'm starving."

Walking with her to the house, he caught a whiff of her perfume in the breeze, a light delicate floral scent that teased his nostrils. "Why didn't you say so? We could have stopped to get a bite to eat in town."

She shook her head. "Not necessary. This fried chicken will do just fine. There may even be some left for you."

He chuckled. "So, you're willing to share? That's mighty generous of you."

"Anything but the wings. They're my favorite."

"Sounds good to me. I'm strictly a leg man." Then he realized he was staring at her legs. He cleared his throat and moved toward the door, pulling his spare house key from his pocket. But when he reached for the doorknob, it turned easily in his hand and the solid oak door swung open. An uneasy feeling rippled through him.

Josie looked up at him. "Does your granny ever leave without locking the front door?"

"Never." He looked over at her. "Do you suppose—"

"Doris," she finished, saying the name he'd left unspoken. "But that woman wouldn't dare come here, would she? And her truck's nowhere in sight."

Noah raised one eyebrow. "If there's one thing I've learned, it's not to underestimate Doris Dooley. Well, that and to buy some plain boxer shorts. But let's look on the bright side. Maybe she just stopped by to pick up the bedsheet I borrowed."

"Or to make good on her threats to you." She moved toward him. "Don't go in there. Let me check it out first."

"No way," Noah said, moving toward the door. "You wait out here while *I* check out the house."

"I'm coming in with you," she insisted. "We'll have a better chance if it's two against one."

"Not if she brought her pistols. I'm not putting you in that kind of danger."

"It's not your choice to make. I'm a grown woman. I can go wherever I want."

He swore softly under his breath, wishing he

didn't care so much. "All right, but please stay behind me."

"Wait, just a minute." She opened her purse and took out the same canister of hair spray that she'd used to threaten him. "Okay, I'm ready."

He slowly pushed open the front door, wincing at the telltale creak. The first thing he noticed was the mess. Dirty dishes littered the kitchen countertop. A box of soda crackers stood open on the dining room table, surrounded by empty soda cans. The hairs on the back of his neck rose. Something was very wrong. Granny had never left a mess like this.

He glanced at Josie, then silently nodded toward the living room, where the television blared. At least the noise had probably masked their entrance, giving them the advantage of surprise.

"Looks like Doris has made herself at home," she whispered.

A shadow fell across the kitchen threshold and Josie squeaked a warning. Noah tensed, pushing her back behind him.

The next moment, a strange man walked through the open doorway. He took one look at them, then staggered against the wall, dropping the half-eaten raspberry muffin in his hand as he grabbed his chest. "Jeez, you scared the crap out of me."

"Miles!" Josie cried out, rounding Noah to hurry toward the man. "What are you doing here?"

Noah stared at the man in disbelief. Miles Dooley looked nothing like he expected. He stood about six feet tall and wore wire-rimmed glasses. His unruly brown hair almost reached his shoulders and made him look like a goofy professor.

And completely harmless.

Miles pushed himself away from the wall, then set his muffin on the table. "Lou contacted me a few hours ago. She told me that you were looking for me, along with some guy named Noah Tanner, and then she gave me this address."

"I'm Noah," he said, stepping forward. "So, you broke into my house and made yourself at home?"

Miles eyes widened in dismay. "Of course not. The front door was unlocked, and it was so hot outside, I decided just to wait in here for you." He looked between the two of them. "You were looking for me, right?"

"Yes," Josie said, placing herself between Noah and Miles. "And we're both happy you're here. Right, Noah?"

He met her gaze. "Sure."

"But I don't understand," Josie said to Miles. "Why didn't you return any of my calls or texts?"

Miles shook his head. "Doris and I had a big fight. She took my phone, so I didn't receive any of your messages. I've been using a burner. I didn't even realize you were in town until I got that message from Lou."

Noah watched Josie move closer to him, her face etched with concern. "Where have you been staying?"

"Here and there," Miles said. "I've tried not to overstay my welcome. I don't want to be a burden to anyone. I was hoping to reconcile with Doris by now, but she's been pretty unreasonable lately."

"Well, you can stay here with us. There's plenty of room. Right, Noah?"

Noah didn't like the idea of this stranger roaming around his house, but what choice did he have? Miles was the key to getting Josie's cat back and finding that will. And the guy did look pretty harmless. "Sure," he said at last.

Miles looked confused. "Us? Are you two... together?"

Josie looked at Noah. "Well—"

"We sure are," Noah said, not yet ready to end their fake romance. "Josie moved in with me."

Without another word, Miles walked out of the kitchen and Josie quickly followed him.

Noah released a sigh of frustration and looked longingly at the bucket of chicken. Telling himself he'd think better on a full stomach, he grabbed a plate out of the cupboard and filled it with chicken, then retrieved a bottle of beer from the refrigerator. When he carried his supper into the living room, he saw Miles now lying on the sofa with his head resting on Josie's lap.

Miles gazed up at Josie, his face pale. "I can't... catch my... breath."

"Noah," Josie said, her blue eyes clouded with concern as she briskly fanned one hand over his pale face. "He's hyperventilating. Can you get that takeout bag the chicken came in?"

Swallowing a groan of frustration, he set his plate on the coffee table, then returned to the kitchen and grabbed the brown paper bag and hurried back into the living room.

"Take slow, deep breaths," she told Miles, taking the bag from Noah and placing it over his mouth. She looked over at Noah. "This used to happen a lot when he visited us in Austin. He's very... sensitive."

She continued to hold the paper bag over Miles' mouth until his breathing returned to normal. "Are you feeling better now?"

Miles pushed the bag away, then stared up into her eyes. "You saved my life."

Josie smiled. "Noah's the one who got the paper bag."

Miles scowled; his mouth rimmed with fried chicken crumbs. "Is he still here?"

Noah swallowed a mouthful of chicken. "Hey, don't thank me."

"Okay, I won't." Miles gazed up at Josie. "Can I get you something to eat?"

She looked longingly at Noah's plate. "That fried chicken looks delicious. But you don't have to go to any trouble. I can get it myself."

Miles leaped off the sofa. "No trouble at all. I'll be right back."

Noah licked his fingers, then settled back in the chair with his beer. "I almost wish it *had* been Doris."

"Don't say that!" Josie whispered. "He might hear you. And we need his help."

He wanted to argue, but she was right. That's why they'd been desperate to find him. But couldn't Josie see that the man was in love with her? It was so obvious to him. On the other hand, Miles' presence would be better than a cold shower to keep Noah from giving in to temptation.

"Okay," he said at last. "Miles is welcome to stay here."

As if on cue, Miles returned to the living room with a plate for Josie, setting it on the coffee table in front of her. "Enjoy."

She stared in dismay at her plate. "What is this?"

"Radicchio and spinach leaves. No dressing. Very low-calorie. I tossed the rest of that bucket of chicken in the trash. It's full of unhealthy fats and additives. That way you won't be tempted."

At the moment, she looked ready to toss the salad greens right in Miles' face. Noah tried not to laugh. "It is hard to resist temptation."

"It certainly is," she agreed, a wry smile curving her mouth.

He couldn't help but smile back at her. He'd never met anyone quite like Josie before, although he couldn't quite figure out how she was different from other women. Other than the fact that she knew how to hot-wire a car and jimmy a lock with a paper clip. Hardly the typical traits of the girl-next-door type.

Josie Reid made him more than a little curious. Although, he knew instinctively that a man could lose his head around her. Or his clothes. Which under different circumstances might not be so bad.

Unfortunately, he couldn't take that kind of chance.

Miles scowled, looking back and forth between the two of them. "Is there something going on here that I should know about?"

"Not a thing, Miles," Noah said, tipping up his beer bottle. "Not a thing."

"Then I guess we should talk about why I'm really here." Miles took a deep breath. "I left Doris."

Josie slowly set down her fork. "I'm sorry, Miles. I'm sure that wasn't easy for you."

He nodded, then reached for her hand, giving it a squeeze. "I knew you'd understand. She was just so upset about Aunt Loretta that she wasn't thinking straight. One day, shortly after the funeral, a moving company showed up at our rental house. That's when I learned she'd hired them to move us into Loretta's home here in Calamity." He shook his head. "It just wasn't right, but she wouldn't listen to reason. She's convinced that Aunt Loretta wrote me out of her new will."

"Do you think she did?" Noah asked bluntly.

Miles shook his head. "Shortly before she died, Aunt Loretta told me that I'd been taken care of, even though I don't need her money. But Doris..." His voice trailed off as he looked over at Josie. "Doris just isn't a trusting person."

"You mean, she doesn't trust *me*," Josie said. "She made that perfectly clear when she stole my cat."

Miles winced. "I heard about that. I'm so sorry. I wish there was something I could do."

Josie glanced over at Noah, then squared her shoulders. "Actually, there is. If you could find a way to lure Doris out of the house to give us enough time to get

Baby and find that will, we can finally honor Loretta's last wishes."

He winced. "Lure? That sounds so... devious."

Noah leaned forward. "If you truly want to help your wife, this would be the best way to do it. You can call her from here and set up a date with her."

Miles rose to his feet, his expression unreadable. "I don't know. You're asking me to trick my wife. I need some time to think."

Josie stood up. "That's perfectly understandable. Why don't you sleep on it, and we can discuss this in the morning."

Miles nodded. "That sounds good. I am tired. And it's time to take my medication." He turned to Noah. "Do you have a bedroom for me to use?"

"The first one at the top of the stairs," Noah told him. "On the left. I can show you the way."

Miles held up one hand. "No, I've got it."

They watched him head toward the staircase and disappear.

Josie turned to Noah, her eyes shining with hope. "I can't believe he just showed up like this, exactly when we needed him."

Noah nodded. "It is... strange. But good, I guess."

"It's wonderful," she exclaimed. "If everything goes well, I could have Baby back as soon as tomorrow!

I could drop off the will at the attorney's office and be on my way to San Antonio by the weekend."

A hollow feeling stirred in the pit of his stomach. He didn't expect her to be so eager to leave Calamity. To leave him. "It might not be that easy."

"We can do this," she said. "I think if we work together, we can do anything."

Chapter Eleven

Long past midnight, Josie took a deep breath, then knocked lightly on Noah's bedroom door. Her bare toes curled on the hardwood floor as she waited for him to reply. When he didn't, she knocked again, only harder this time.

She tried to ignore the pounding of her heart. The stress of the car chase last Saturday, the break-in, Doris holding Noah at gunpoint, and now Miles appearing out of nowhere were obviously all beginning to catch up with her. But even more difficult was pretending to be in love with a man whom she was finding almost impossible to resist.

At last, she heard the sound of a groggy voice, though she couldn't decipher the words. She opened the door to his room and stuck her head inside. "May I come in?"

Noah blinked at the light shining in from the hallway, half sitting up in the bed. "Who is it?"

"Me. Josie."

He blinked again, then pulled the bedclothes up to his neck. "What wrong?"

"Nothing's wrong." She walked into the room, gently closing the door behind her. She moved toward the bed, the hem of her green satin robe swirling around her thighs. "I'm just nervous."

He stared at her, his Adam's apple bobbing in his throat. "About what?"

"About the phone call Miles is going to make to Doris. I think we should write it out for him, like a script. This may be our only shot, so we have to get it right."

"Oh." He relaxed against his pillows, then squinted at the clock on his bedside table. "It's two o'clock in the morning."

"Sorry, I couldn't sleep." She turned toward the door. "I can leave..."

"No, stay. I'm already awake." He rubbed one hand over his jaw, rough with dark whiskers. He regarded her with half-closed eyes. "I like your hair that way."

She laughed softly. "It's a mess. I just got out of bed."

"I know. That's what I like about it."

She moved closer to him, her bare feet padding over the rug. "Are you sure you're awake? You sound different."

When he folded his arms behind his head, the blanket slipped down to reveal the top half of his bare chest. "I'm only half-awake and I'm hoping like hell this is a dream. Of course, if it were a dream, you wouldn't be standing there."

She took a step closer to him, her voice a husky whisper. "What would I be doing?"

He closed his eyes. "Oh, Josie, I can think of a thousand things."

So could she. Especially with him lying there in the partial shadows, his voice rough and low. It sent a primitive shiver through her. She'd heard the term "animal attraction" before, but she'd never really understood it until now.

But she wanted more than lust between them. She might even want love. But Noah had made it clear that he wasn't interested in anything long term.

"Is one of those things planning what Miles should say on the call?" she asked playfully, breaking the intensely sensual moment between them.

He opened his eyes, a wry smile tipping up one corner of his mouth. "No, but it's probably the safest one."

"I've been thinking about it and thought we could

rehearse. Maybe even write a short script for him to follow."

"At this hour? Sorry, but I'm not thinking too clearly at the moment."

"That makes two of us. But Miles could disappear again, so the sooner we put this plan in motion, the better. If we figure it out tonight, maybe we can convince him to call Doris first thing in the morning."

"I suppose you have a point." Noah sat up farther in the bed, the movement causing him to scrape his shoulder blade against the headboard. He grimaced at the contact. "I'm going to hurt myself before this is over."

He could hurt her, too, she suddenly realized. She'd come to like him quite well in the brief time they'd known each other. And she didn't take to strangers easily.

Josie took a small notepad and pen from the pocket of her robe, then sat on the edge of the bed. "Let me write it down." She nibbled on her thumbnail, wanting to choose just the right words. Because if Doris sensed something was off, she might never leave the house. "Let's start with, 'Hello, Doris, this is Miles.'"

"Very creative," he quipped, watching her jot it down on the notepad.

"Okay, maybe you should tell me what a man would say?"

His gaze moved over her face. "I think it makes more sense to write down what a woman would want to hear. Especially a woman like Doris."

"You're right. Give me a minute."

Josie sensed Noah was watching her as she began to write in the notepad. For several minutes, the scratching of the pen moving across the paper was the only sound in the room. At last, she put the pen down. "Okay, I'm done."

"I think the best thing to do is make this call short and to the point. The longer he keeps her on the line, the more likely he'll screw up the call."

"How's this? Doris, this is Miles. I've missed you. I know we have a lot to talk about, but I'd like to do it face-to-face. Will you meet me for coffee at Blue Moon at noon today?"

Noah laced his fingers behind his head, the movement flexing the muscles in his bare chest. "Not bad. But it's missing something."

"You told me to keep it short and to the point."

"I know, but we need a hook. Something that will make it impossible for her to refuse to meet him." He snapped his fingers. "How about this. Doris, I just got some test results back from my doctor and there's something you need to know."

Josie covered her face with both hands, trying to conceal her laughter.

"Well?"

Her body shook, her face still concealed from him.

He sighed. "That bad, huh?"

She drew her hands away, unable to conceal her laughter any longer. "I can't imagine anything worse."

He scowled, then leaned over her, propping his chin in his hand. "Those aren't exactly the words a man wants to hear from the woman lying in his bed."

"Sorry, but it's the truth."

He shifted on the mattress, his hand accidentally grazing her collarbone.

She sucked in her breath and Noah's own breathing hitched at the contact. When she stared into his eyes, he suddenly realized how very close he was to her. Only scant millimeters away from her mouth. Before he could stop to think, he leaned forward, lightly brushing her lips with his own.

Her arms curled around his neck as he deepened the kiss, a low moan emanating from his throat. His hand found her waist, smoothing the supple fabric of her chemise as he molded her hip. She was irresistible. And in that moment, she was all his.

The thought doused his ardor like a splash of chilly water.

He broke the kiss, his body screaming in protest. She blinked up at him, looking so soft and sexy he could barely stand it.

"That was some goodnight kiss," she said huskily. She sat up and rose off the bed, wobbling just a little. She steadied herself against the mattress. "Do you want me to tuck you in?"

"No, thanks. I'm a big boy."

"I can tell," she said with a small smile as she glided out the bedroom door.

He plopped back against the pillows, furious with himself for giving in to temptation. She didn't need any more complications in her life. And he didn't want to risk losing his heart to a woman who was eager to put Calamity in her rearview mirror.

Noah got up and closed the door behind her, half wishing it had a lock. Not to keep her out, but to keep him in.

It was going to be a very long night.

The night got even longer when Noah awoke to a bright, blinding white light shining in his face a couple of hours later. He squinted, shielding his eyes with his hand and half rising off his pillow.

The light wavered. "Are you awake?"

Miles.

He swallowed a groan. "I am now. What the hell are you doing up at this hour?"

"Twenty dollars."

Noah sat up in bed. "You're not making any sense. Are you sleepwalking? Or did you forget to take your medication?"

"My counselor said I don't have to take it every day anymore. I'm making wonderful progress." He shone the flashlight directly in Noah's eyes. "You look tired."

"Turn that damn thing off! Of course, I'm tired." He glanced at the illuminated screen of his cell phone. "It's four o'clock in the morning!"

Miles switched off the flashlight, then flipped on the overhead light. "Man, and I thought Doris was cranky whenever I woke her up in the middle of the night. I just wanted to make sure we could talk in private."

Noah winced at the brightness. "What do you want?"

"Twenty bucks."

"I'm not giving you money."

"No, I mean I want to give *you* twenty bucks."

"For what?" Noah rubbed his eyes, trying to make sense of this convoluted conversation. It was hard enough to comprehend Miles' ramblings when he was fully conscious.

"For leaving. In fact, now would be a perfect time."

"You want to pay me to leave my own ranch?"

"Just temporarily. In fact, I'll throw in five bucks as an incentive if you're out of here in the next fifteen minutes."

"Why?"

"Because I'm a naturally generous guy. Just ask anybody." Miles hesitated. "Well, on second thought, don't ask my cousin Vance. He's still upset about leaving that winning raffle ticket at my place. Don't ask Carl at work, either. The kid who delivers the newspaper wouldn't be a good reference. But I think almost anyone else would agree."

Noah closed his eyes, wondering if this was a nightmare. "Miles, I am not taking your money."

"You mean you'll leave for free?"

"No. I'm not leaving. Period." He lay back down and drew the blanket over his shoulders. "Good night."

Miles began pacing the room. "Thirty bucks."

"I'm going to sleep now."

"Thirty-one. That's my highest offer."

Noah cracked one eye. "Why are you so anxious for me to leave?"

"Because you're cramping my style, Tanner.

There's a gorgeous woman living in this house, and I'd like a chance to romance her in private."

"Romance her?" Noah laughed out loud. "You're married!"

Miles scowled at him. "I don't think it's going to last. I'm afraid Doris won't take me back this time."

Noah shook his head. "Look, I'm sorry for your problems. But you and Doris can work it out later—after Josie gets her cat back and settles this matter with the will. If you care about her at all..." His voice trailed off, and he pushed the blanket off his chest, feeling uncomfortably warm.

"Thirty-two dollars and fifty cents," Miles offered, then he folded his arms across his chest. "You know, it's not like I consider you a real threat. Everybody in Calamity knows your relationships with women are shorter than the life span of a gnat."

The contention irritated him, even if it was true. "Then what's the problem?"

"You're a distraction. I saw the way Josie was staring at you tonight. Like she'd never seen a few muscles before."

"Miles, it's late. I'm tired and you look like you're about to start hyperventilating again."

"Thirty-five dollars. That's my final offer. Take it or leave it."

"I'll leave it." Noah yawned. "Could you turn off the light on your way out?"

Miles pressed his lips together, then headed for the door. "I hope you don't regret it, Tanner." He flipped the switch, plunging the room into darkness. "I really hope you don't regret it."

Chapter Twelve

The next morning, Noah opened up Blue Moon Coffee Shop at six a.m. sharp and got everything set up by the time the first employees arrived for their shift. Then he walked into the back office, shut the door, and promptly fell asleep at the desk.

At seven a.m., a knock sounded at the door. "Hey, Tanner," a deep male voice called. "You in there?"

Noah lifted his head off the desk. "Keep it down out there. Some of us are trying to sleep."

The door opened and Trey Booker, a stocky African American deputy only a couple of years older than Noah, walked inside holding a large espresso. "I heard you've started pushing my favorite legal stimulant and are moonlighting as a barista." He took a seat in the nearest chair. "But I had to see it to believe it."

Two years ago, Trey had headed up a complex

criminal investigation involving a ring of cattle rustlers and had used Noah's knowledge of the cattle business to trap his targets. The two had become fast friends, sharing a common interest in horses, beautiful women, and the Dallas Cowboys.

"It's temporary," Noah assured him. "I'm filling in while Shelby and Taylor are attending some conference. But what are you doing up so early?"

"Just heading off to work." Booker held up the large foam cup. "I stop here every morning for my caffeine fix on the way into the station. There's nothing like a cup of espresso and a couple of chocolate biscotti to start the day."

"What, no donuts?"

"That's an ugly stereotype." He laughed, setting his cup on the table next to him. "The sheriff's department is much classier than people think. Certainly, classier than some cowboys I know."

"Shouldn't you be out fighting crime?"

"Man, you are cranky this morning."

"I didn't get much sleep last night."

Trey grinned. "I should have known. I heard you've got a new girlfriend living with you. I was a little surprised after what happened with Amber, but you've been alone for a while now."

In truth, it felt like a hell of a long time. Longer than Noah wanted to admit. That probably explained his strong attraction to Josie. Abstinence obviously didn't agree with him.

Although technically, he had had a beautiful woman in his bed last night. She just hadn't stayed there. "Just living up to my reputation. Or so the ladies tell me."

Trey snorted. "Man, you are so full of bull crap. I'm just waiting for the day some woman brings you to your knees."

"Spoken like a married man. How is Mina, anyway?"

Trey beamed. "Beautiful, sexy, and six weeks pregnant."

Noah blinked, surprised one of his old bachelor buddies had transformed so quickly, and apparently easily, into a proud husband and father-to-be. "Hey, that's great! You must be really excited."

Trey nodded. "And scared to death. But I've felt that way ever since I met Mina, so I'm starting to get used to it."

"I've been feeling the same way," Noah admitted, "ever since I met Josie."

Trey knitted his brow. "Is that your new girlfriend's name?"

He nodded. "Josie Reid. She's from Austin."

Trey leaned forward in his chair. "Oh, I've heard a lot about her. Seems she made quite an impression at

Shawn and Amber's wedding reception. Blond, built, and beautiful from all accounts."

"That's the one," Noah said.. The rumor mill had done just what he'd expected, letting everyone in Calamity know that Noah Tanner was no longer a poor, jilted cowboy.

Trey nodded his approval. "She sounds like quite the dish."

Inexplicably, Noah felt a burst of masculine pride. "I've never met anyone like her. Unfortunately, she's been having some trouble with a woman named Doris Dooley."

"She's not the only one. I hear you've been posing as an insurance agent?"

Noah blinked at the sudden shift of subject. Though it shouldn't have surprised him since he knew it was the way Booker worked his investigations. He'd just never been on the receiving end before. "I take it you've heard from Doris."

Booker pulled a small memo pad out of his shirt pocket. "Doris Dooley came into the station the other day. Apparently, she was quite upset."

"She's not the only one," he muttered under his breath.

"She claims you entered her home under false pretenses."

"And?"

Booker studied him for a moment. "And that you took your clothes off."

"What!"

"And stole a bedsheet."

Noah clenched his jaw. "She's twisting this all out of proportion."

Booker arched a brow. "So, you're saying none of that happened?"

He wished he could say it. Unfortunately, everything Doris had claimed was true. She'd just conveniently omitted a few pertinent details.

"Doris invited me into her house to discuss insurance," he began.

"Since when did you start rounding up insurance clients instead of cattle? I didn't even know you'd gotten into the insurance business."

He could tell the truth—or he could protect Josie. "I'm branching out."

Booker snorted. "Give me a break, Tanner. I'm trying to help you here. Doris Dooley hasn't pressed any charges yet, but she's seriously considering it. I also heard she's thinking about filing sexual harassment charges against you."

"That's ridiculous." Noah looked at the deputy. "Would you believe me if I told you she held me at gunpoint, made me strip, then confiscated my clothes?"

Trey looked at him skeptically as he sat back in the chair, tapping his pen against the memo pad. "Maybe. First, tell me what Josie has to do with all of this."

"Doris has been harassing her. Last Saturday, she stole her cat. I was just trying to help her get it back."

"Rescuing damsels in distress? That doesn't sound like your style. You're more the kiss-and-run type."

The assessment made him bristle. "Gee, thanks."

"Hey, it's nothing personal. I just call 'em like I see 'em."

Noah fiddled with the paper clip on top of the desk. "Well, I'm not planning to kiss Josie," he said. *Not again, if he could help it.* "But I am sticking close to her, at least until she doesn't need me anymore. This Doris is a wacko."

"Just be careful, Noah." Booker rose to his feet. "Even wackos have rights. If Doris Dooley decides to file charges against you, I'm not sure I can dissuade her. You might want to consult a good defense attorney."

Noah closed his eyes with a frustrated sigh. "Not long ago, my life was perfectly normal. Then I meet Josie Reid and all hell breaks loose."

Booker laughed as he moved toward the door. "Spoken like a man falling in love."

The deputy was out the door before Noah could contradict him. *Falling in love?* No way. Not possible. Then he thought about their hot kiss last night. And the fact that he couldn't stop thinking about her. No woman had ever had that effect on him before, not even his ex-fiancée.

Did that mean he was falling in love with Josie?

He plucked a pen off the desk and studied the receipts in front of him, trying to push her out of his mind. A man couldn't fall in love with a woman against his will.

No matter how much he might want to.

Josie sat curled up in an armchair in Noah's living room, trying to concentrate on the manual the museum had sent her before she left Austin. She wanted to memorize it before she arrived for her new job, so she'd be ready to hit the ground running. Josie loved reading about Texas history but was having trouble concentrating today.

She'd given the script to Miles this morning, and he'd promised to call Doris when he was finished with breakfast. But he'd apparently left the ranch while she was in the shower.

By the time she'd dressed and headed back downstairs, Miles was gone and so was his car that he'd parked on the side of the house. Now she was waiting to hear from him and trying not to worry.

Josie turned her attention back to the manual. "Good cataloguing techniques are vital for orderly maintenance of historical records and artifacts," she read aloud. The words blurred as her mind drifted to the night before. Noah had excellent technique. She closed her eyes, reliving that kiss, her body tingling just as it had done then. He was good. He was very, very good.

She opened her eyes and cleared her throat, finding her place on the page. "Technique can be taught, but a true historian needs something more. Patience, and a talent for spotting hidden treasures."

Did she have talent? Lately, it seemed she only had a talent for finding trouble. Years ago, she'd discovered an entirely different assortment of talents. The kind that required a certain amount of charm, the nerve of a high-stakes gambler, and the ability to think on her feet.

Noah was charming in his own way. She just hoped Miles could summon enough charm to lure Doris away from the house. They'd probably be lucky if Doris hadn't already figured out their ploy and decided to take revenge. Then her smile faded.

Would her cat suffer for it?

She swallowed hard as all the worries she'd shoved to the back of her mind came rushing back. Was Baby hungry? Thirsty? Afraid? The only thing that gave her solace was the fact that her cat was a scrapper. She'd managed to survive a long time on the streets before Josie had found her and taken her to the animal shelter.

Her hand tightened on the manual. She'd find Baby again, no matter what it took. Her search had started again this morning when she'd called all the animal shelters in Calamity and the surrounding towns, hoping Doris might have decided to drop Baby off at one of them. But none of the cats had matched her description of Baby.

Still, she'd left her name and cell phone number, just in case. She'd also posted Baby's photo all over social media and even placed a notice in the newspaper's lost and found section, offering a reward.

She took a deep breath, forcing her concentration back on the book in her lap. "Curators of historical artifacts and records preserve the past for current and future generations. Failure to maintain historical items properly can lead to disaster."

She reached up to turn the page. *Disaster* pretty much summed up her trip to Calamity. Nothing had gone right, except for meeting Noah. She didn't know where she'd be right now if he hadn't stepped up to help her. Of course, he'd made her strike a bargain first, but her role as his fake girlfriend had been fairly easy so far.

Leaving him would be the hard part. Her heart sank at the thought of never seeing him again. But maybe she wasn't thinking clearly, given everything that had happened. Once she got Baby back and Loretta's handwritten will in the hands of her attorney, she could put all of this behind her and start her new life in San Antonio.

She could finally have a forever home of her own.

And wasn't that what she'd wanted for as long as she could remember?

Josie turned her attention back to the manual, determined to think positive. That was when she saw it. A small, sealed envelope stuck in the crease of the book. She picked it up and turned it over in her hand, her breath catching in her throat as she saw her name inscribed on the front in Loretta's unique handwriting.

Her throat tightened as she stared at the envelope, wondering when Loretta had put it there. Josie had often studied the manual while at Loretta's bedside, never wanting to leave her alone for too long. Loretta must have put it there when Josie was out of the room.

With her hands shaking, Josie broke the seal and pulled out a page of Loretta's signature pink stationery.

My dearest Josie,

You are the daughter of my heart, and I will love you

forever. Thank you for coming into my life at just the right time. And for agreeing to take the Reid name as your own. You've worked so hard to earn your degree and to build the life that you want. Never let your fears get in the way of your dreams. And never be afraid to dream the impossible.

Love, Loretta

Tears stung her eyes as she read the letter again, then pressed it to her chest. Loretta was the mother she'd never had—and had always longed for. She also knew Josie better than anyone because she did have an impossible dream—and it wasn't in San Antonio.

It was a dream that hadn't even existed until she'd arrived in Calamity and jumped into a stranger's pickup truck.

Was that fate?

The front door opened, and Noah walked inside the house. She hastily tucked Loretta's note back in the envelope and returned it to its place inside the manual.

"Oh, good, you're still here." Noah put down the shopping bag in his hand. "How did the phone call with Doris go?"

Josie shrugged. "I don't know if Miles has even called her yet. He said he was going to, but then he left the ranch while I was in the shower. I'm hoping he'll let us know." She studied his expression. "Did you want me for something?"

He gave her a lazy smile. "Now that's a loaded question."

Her gaze fell to his mouth and her lips tingled in response. It was his fault for looking so irresistible in black denim jeans, a fitted gray T-shirt, and a black cowboy hat.

"I need a picture of your cat," he said at last.

She looked up from his mouth. "Baby? Why?"

"I'm going to put an ad in the newspaper and offer a reward. I thought a picture would be the best way to identify her."

Now it was her turn to smile. "Thanks, but it's already taken care of. I placed an ad in the classifieds about an hour ago."

"Then I guess it's true what they say—great minds really do think alike."

If his mind was in the same place as hers, he wouldn't be standing there right now. Or wearing clothes. Josie abruptly sat down again, overwhelmed by a sudden surge of desire. She'd been attracted to men before, but the intensity of her reaction to Noah surprised her.

Noah grabbed an antique piano stool from the corner of the room. "There's another reason I wanted to see you."

Her heart did a ridiculous somersault at his words. “Oh?”

He pulled the stool closer to her chair, then straddled it. “I want to apologize for last night.”

She smiled. “Don’t worry. You did your best. I’ve probably just had a lot more practice at that sort of thing.”

He arched a brow. “Have you?”

Josie bit her tongue, wishing she’d kept her mouth shut. The last thing she wanted to do was get into a detailed discussion of her past. That would just give him one more reason not to fall in love with her.

She waved the subject away with her hand. “Forget it, Noah. These things happen.”

He nodded thoughtfully. “You’re right. It was late and we were both tired. I assure you it will never happen again.”

She stared at him, thoroughly confused.

“We’ll just forget it ever happened,” he said. “After all, it was only a kiss.”

Heat burned up her cheeks. She’d read him all wrong. He wasn’t apologizing to her for his work on the script. He was apologizing for kissing her!

Even worse, he’d just promised it would never happen again.

“Is something wrong?” he asked, studying her. “You look flushed.”

"No. Of course not." She flapped her hand in front of her face. "It's just a little warm in here."

He nodded. "I'll adjust the air conditioner."

She stood up, tucking the manual firmly under her arm. "Well, if that's all, I have some things I need to do."

"Just one more thing."

She moved toward the door, not looking at him. "Yes?"

"I bought something for you." He walked toward her, then picked up the shopping bag he'd dropped by the door.

"Here," he said, shoving it into her hands. "I really hope you like it."

"Noah, you shouldn't have..." she began, but he was already out the door.

She held up the shopping bag, noting the familiar name of the boutique located just around the corner from the Blue Moon Coffee Shop. She opened it and pulled out her present.

It was a bathrobe. A floor-length, long-sleeved green terry cloth robe. With a zipper from hem to neck. It was the ugliest robe she'd ever seen, even if the color did match her nightgown.

And she couldn't have been happier about it.

Noah might be resistant to her charms, but he obviously wasn't immune. Otherwise, he wouldn't go to so much trouble to cover them up. She hugged the robe to her, hope taking the place of despair. If everything went according to plan the next few days, she'd find that will, rescue Baby, and follow Loretta's advice by pursuing an impossible dream.

Never say never.

Chapter Thirteen

That night, Josie made lasagna for supper, splurged on a bottle of full-bodied Chianti, and wore her sexiest dress—a black strapless number that made breathing problematic. She only forgot one thing.

Miles.

He walked through the back door just as she pulled the lasagna pan out of the oven. Then he took one look at her and froze in his tracks. "Wow."

"Hello, Miles," she said, setting the hot pan on a trivet in the center of the table. Disappointment knifed through her, but she tried hard not to show it. Miles might be a little flaky, but he was also sensitive and a good friend. "I thought you had plans with Doris tonight."

"I did, but she canceled. She's not feeling well." He

leaned over and inhaled the lasagna. "Smells great. I'll bet you didn't know this is my favorite dish."

"Actually, it's Loretta's recipe. I just hope I do it justice. She was an awesome cook."

"She sure was," Miles agreed, growing somber.

Josie didn't mention that she'd done some research on Noah by visiting his granny. In the span of an afternoon, she'd learned that Noah liked lasagna, old black-and-white westerns, and leggy brunettes. Not necessarily in that order. She'd been hoping to discover a few of his other likes and dislikes over an intimate candlelight dinner.

Miles pulled out a chair and sat down, snapping open the white linen napkin she'd spent so much time artfully folding. Then he tucked the napkin into the front of his shirt. "When do we eat?"

"It's ready now," she said, resigning herself to dinner for three. She walked over to the refrigerator to retrieve the farro salad. "Would you please tell Noah it's time to eat?"

Miles leaned toward the doorway and shouted, "Hey, Tanner, it's time to eat."

"Thanks," she said dryly, setting the salad on the table.

She turned just as Noah walked into the kitchen. He stopped abruptly and stared. His eyes took the slow route from her head to her feet and back again. "What's all this?"

"I just wanted to thank you for your gift. That's why I made supper tonight."

Miles reached for a slice of garlic bread. "Gift? What gift?"

Josie looked at Noah and noted that he was still staring. She took that as a good sign. "He bought me a nice warm terry cloth robe."

Miles wrinkled his nose. "Warm? In the middle of September?"

"It's the thought that counts," she said, setting another place at the table. "Go ahead and sit down, Noah, before it gets cold."

He stood rooted to the spot. "Does the robe fit?"

"It's perfect. I'll model it for you later." She poured three glasses of wine, then set the bottle back on the table.

He swallowed hard. "I'd really like to see you put it on now."

Miles nodded, waving his fork in the air. "You know, that's not a bad idea. It's already warm in here from the oven. If you put on a big robe, it will be just like sitting in a sauna. That's a wonderful way to relax." He half rose out of his chair. "I'll go get it for you."

She pushed down hard on his narrow shoulder. "I'm not wearing the robe."

"Are you sure?" Miles asked her. "It's no trouble."

"Eat, Miles," she ordered, wondering if she'd overdone it with the dress. Vamping really wasn't her style. At least, not anymore.

She turned around to see Noah holding her chair out for her. "Thank you."

"You look... amazing." His fingers brushed against her bare shoulder as she sat down. His touch electrified her, and she realized Miles was right—the kitchen had turned into a sauna.

Noah sat down across the table from her. "Everything looks delicious."

A blush crept up her neck when she realized he wasn't looking at the food. He was still staring at her. She picked up her fork. "I hope you like it."

He followed suit. "It's almost irresistible."

Almost. Josie reached for her wine, studying Noah through her lashes. He ate with an enthusiasm that surprised her. Intrigued her. As she sipped her wine, she wondered what it would be like to be on the receiving end of all that intensity.

Miles forked up a bite of lasagna, gooey with melted mozzarella. "I heard in town that your friend Shawn and his wife just left for their honeymoon."

"Good." Noah caught her gaze and held it. "I

hope they have great time." For a long moment, it was almost as if they were alone in the room. His hungry expression left no doubt about what he'd like to be doing right now. Then he turned his attention back to his plate and she wondered if she'd just imagined it.

"I wonder if they're truly happy," Miles pondered, picking up his wineglass. "They probably don't have any regrets yet."

"Yet?" Josie echoed.

He shrugged. "Let's face it. They caused a bit of scandal—at Noah's expense. They met, fell in love, and got hitched within the span of a few months."

"You don't even know them," Josie said, growing annoyed with the conversation.

She still wasn't sure how Noah felt about his ex-fiancée dumping him. Was he still in love with Amber? Had Noah kissed her on the rebound?

Miles nodded. "They sure got married quick."

"She's crazy about him," Josie said. "And he's even crazier about her. Anyone could see that at the reception."

"And they saved me from making the biggest mistake of my life," Noah said. "It took me a long time to see it that way, but it's true."

"My parents only knew each other for two weeks when my father proposed," Miles said. "They'll be celebrating their thirtieth wedding anniversary next month."

"Then they're the exception, not the rule." Noah helped himself to another serving of lasagna. "My father married my mother after only knowing her for ten months. She left eight years later."

Her gaze softened. "I'm sorry that happened to you."

"It happens. Love can't always survive secrets. And there's no way two people can learn each other's secrets in the space of a few weeks. Most of the time, it takes years."

"Years?" Josie's grip tightened on the stem of her wineglass. She had a few secrets of her own. Secrets she hadn't planned to share with anyone—including her future husband. "Isn't that a little extreme?"

"Not as extreme as marriage to a virtual stranger."

She rolled her eyes. "Your reasoning is totally impractical—for a woman who wants children, anyway. She can't wait years if her biological clock is ticking."

Miles perked up. "Dooley men are very virile. We can handle any clock around. Just in case you're interested."

Noah glowered at him. "How generous of you."

Josie suppressed a smile. "Thanks for the offer, Miles. I'm only twenty-five, so it's hardly an emergency situation yet." She paused a beat, impulsively deciding to spill one of her secrets. "But I do want six kids."

Noah choked on his lasagna. Miles reached over and pounded him on the back until he recovered. Noah stared at her disbelief. "Six kids?"

"Three girls and three boys would be nice, but I'm flexible."

"I think there's another word for it." He picked up his wineglass. "*Six kids.* You'd have enough for your very own volleyball team."

"I love volleyball."

"I'm a baseball fan myself," Noah said. "But what about your husband? Won't he have any say in the matter?"

"I suppose so, since it would be hard to make six babies without him." She knew she was goading him, but she couldn't help it. He was so cute when he was flustered. "I'd need a man with a lot of stamina."

Miles settled back in his chair. "I've been lifting weights."

"He'll need more than stamina," Noah said, tossing his napkin on top of his empty plate. "He'll need his head examined."

She bristled. "Are you saying a man would have to be crazy to want to marry me?"

"Of course not. I'm simply saying..." His voice trailed off as his gaze fell to her mouth.

"Yes?" she prodded.

His gaze met hers and his voice dropped to a low, husky whisper. "You're definitely driving me crazy."

That was when Josie decided her dinner party was a smashing success.

* * *

On Wednesday afternoon, Noah sat in the office at Blue Moon Coffee Shop, going over the receipts from the day before. He'd been up before dawn to do all the ranch chores, then headed into Calamity to open the coffee shop. Some of his work on the ranch was piling up, and just this morning he'd discovered that a raccoon had chewed through the roof of an old shed and was now taking up residence there.

But that wasn't his only problem.

His fake romance with Josie was driving him crazy. Spending day and night with her in the same house was taking its toll. He couldn't eat. Couldn't sleep. Couldn't stop thinking about her.

Worst of all, he kept forgetting all the reasons why she was completely wrong for him. She was a beautiful, intelligent, and fascinating woman. She could make him laugh. And she had a hidden strength that inexorably drew him to her.

But she was also leaving Calamity soon and had no

plans to return. Which was exactly what he'd wanted when he'd proposed their fake romance. It was the perfect temporary setup since he was determined to remain a bachelor. So why did the thought of never seeing her again make him feel sick inside?

He looked around at the four white walls of the tiny office. A small square window looked out on the gravel parking lot at the back of the coffee shop.

That was the question. How the hell was he supposed to know the answer? Especially when time was running out.

He'd always sworn to himself he wouldn't make the same mistake as his parents. He wouldn't fall in love with someone who as all wrong for him. It just wasn't worth the pain. But the thought of her leaving was causing him pain too. A deep heartache he'd never experienced before—not even after Amber left him.

Noah swore softly under his breath and massaged his throbbing temple. He looked at the wall calendar. The date she was scheduled to start her new job in San Antonio was coming up quickly. All he had to do was tough it out a little longer, and maybe this torture would finally end. That and continue taking a lot of cold showers.

The office door opened, and Miles stuck his head inside. "One of the toilets in the men's room is plugged up."

"Again?"

Miles shrugged. "Maybe you didn't use the plunger right the last time."

Noah had brought Miles with him to the coffee shop this morning, just to give him something to do. Miles seemed to enjoy chatting with the customers and keeping the place neat and tidy. Almost too neat and tidy—Miles seemed obsessed with any minor problem he could find.

Noah had already used the plunger three times in the last three hours. And on a different toilet each time. If he didn't know better, he'd think someone was deliberately stuffing them with toilet paper just to cause him trouble.

"You'd better hurry," Miles said with a smirk. "There's a line forming."

Noah leaned back in his chair, staring him down. "Why don't you take care of it this time?"

Miles stood in the doorway, folding his arms across his narrow chest. "I have a science degree, but I have no experience with plumbing. I'm doing the best I can to help out around here, but I suppose next you'll want me to take the kitchen sink apart."

The back of his neck prickled. "Is something wrong with the kitchen sink?"

"Someone dropped a couple of forks down the garbage disposal. It's really making a racket."

Noah struggled to hold on to his temper. He knew if he started yelling, Miles would threaten to call Josie again. The last thing he wanted was Josie thinking he couldn't handle a few minor problems. Or even a major problem. Like Miles.

"It's not going to work," Noah warned him.

Miles blinked innocently at him. "What's not going to work?"

"All these little games you've been playing. Like plugging the toilets and the garbage disposal here at the coffee shop. And hiding the television remote control at my house. Don't you think that's just a little childish?"

"You're the one playing games. Only you're playing them with Josie. It's obvious she's crazy about you. And you just keep leading her on!"

Noah's jaw clenched. "I am not leading her on."

Miles rolled his eyes. "Oh, please! You came down to breakfast without a shirt on this morning. How am I supposed to compete with that?"

"First of all, you're a married man, so you shouldn't be competing for anyone." Noah stood up. "And second, you're the one who took my shirts out of the laundry room and hid them in the broom closet."

"I already told you, I thought they were cleaning rags."

"You're wasting your time, Miles. Josie and I are

just..." His voice trailed off when he realized he was about to admit they'd just been pretending to be in love.

And something told him Miles would spread that news around town as quickly as possible. And the truth was, he'd moved beyond pretending into something deeper. More primal. He tried to think of an appropriate word to describe their relationship. He wouldn't exactly call them friends, even though he did enjoy spending time with her. Enjoyed it way too much for his own peace of mind.

Miles took another step into the room. "Just what?"

"Just trying to get her cat back. You should know as well as anyone how much she loves her cat."

"And I think you're taking advantage of that fact," Miles said. "Just like you're trying every trick in the book to get her into your bed. I've warned her about you, Tanner, but I don't think it's done a hell of a lot of good."

Noah knew he shouldn't ask, but he couldn't help himself. "What do you mean?"

"What do I mean? How about the way she's always gazing at you when you're not looking? Or the way she hangs on your every word? It makes me want to shake some sense into her."

"I think you're exaggerating," Noah said, trying to ignore the warm glow deep inside of him.

"That's what she said when I told her all the bad stuff about you."

He scowled. "What bad stuff?"

"Like the fact that your fiancée left you for your best friend. I've heard the rumors around town. Most folks around here feel sorry for you, but you must have done something pretty bad for them to turn to each other like that."

"You don't know anything about me."

Miles shrugged. "Well, you've got that right. But do you really know Josie? Like the fact that she loves history so much she got a master's degree in the subject. And she's really crazy about Texas history. That she's so thrilled to take the job as curator of a museum in Texas. It's been a dream of hers for a long time."

Noah's irritation began to fade as he realized that Miles was partially right. He didn't know much about Josie. She'd revealed very little about her life to him. Or her dreams. Although she'd been very clear on more than one occasion how eager she was to get to San Antonio.

"So, you need to back off," Miles said. "Sorry if that sounds harsh, but she doesn't need a big, stubborn cowboy making her life any more difficult."

Noah took another step toward him. “I’m not the only one making her life difficult. Your wife is keeping her cat hostage. What are you doing to fix that?”

Miles frowned as he backed away from him. “I’m working on it.”

“Don’t worry about me, Miles. Worry about yourself.” He lowered his voice and took another step closer to him. “Because if the toilets and sinks both here and at the ranch keep plugging up, or any other catastrophe happens around here, I’m coming after you. If any other catastrophe happens with your fingerprints on it, then we’ll see who’s running away.”

Miles’ dark eyes narrowed. “Are you threatening me?”

“Of course not.” Noah would never pick on someone weaker than himself. “I’m just making my position clear. In fact, let’s a call a truce.”

Miles looked skeptical. “A truce?”

He nodded. “We both want what’s best for Josie. Let’s work together to make that happen. Then we never have to see each other again. Deal?”

Miles taut expression relaxed into a smile. “Of course. That’s what I’ve wanted all along.” He leaned forward and lowered his voice a notch.

“But let me ask you a hypothetical question. Suppose someone asked me to give you a message, but I sort of forgot about it. Would that make you mad?”

"Definitely."

"Okay." Miles turned toward the doorway.

"Miles?"

He hesitated with one hand wrapped around the doorframe. "What?"

"Do you have a message for me?"

Miles glanced over his shoulder. "Not if it will make you mad."

"I'll only get mad if you walk out that door without giving it to me."

Miles' left eye twitched. "Josie called."

His pulse picked up. "Called? When?"

"A little while ago. I answered your phone because you were talking to a plumber."

The last time Noah had seen her was this morning when he'd dropped her off at the auto shop to pick up her car. Since then, he'd been hidden away in the office most of the day—when he wasn't unplugging toilets.

"What did she say?"

Miles edged farther out the door. "Are you sure you're not mad?"

"Positive," he said between clenched teeth.

"Well, she wants you to meet her."

He silently counted to ten. "Where and when?"

"At the Tenth Street Tavern," Miles said, one foot out the door. "She wanted you to meet her there an hour ago." Then he fled before Noah could make a move. Which was a good thing because he'd probably have gone for the guy's throat.

The Tenth Street Tavern? Had Miles gotten the message wrong? What would Josie be doing in that place? It was on the edge of the historic district and catered to an eclectic crowd of small-time hoods and local theater buffs.

He glanced out the window. The midafternoon sun shone through, illuminating the dust motes on the oak shutters. Surely, she wouldn't wait there an hour for him without calling. Then another thought occurred to him. What if someone else had shown up? What if Doris had followed her there?

Noah rose slowly to his feet, his stomach knotting from a combination of frustration and fear. He'd told her not to go anywhere without telling him. Naturally, she hadn't listened. She never wore that damn robe he'd bought her, either. When he tracked her down, he definitely planned to set her straight about a few things. But first things first.

He reached for the plunger.

Chapter Fourteen

Josie leaned over the pool table and took aim at the cue ball. Country music twanged out of the jukebox and even though the bar was practically empty, a haze of smoke hung around the pool light just above her. She cued up, shot, and missed.

Her opponent, a guy name Vance, grinned at her. "Oops."

She looked up at him. "Can I have a do-over?"

"No do-overs in the game of pool, babe," he said, shaking his head.

When she'd first arrived at the tavern, Vance had approached Josie and told her all about the custom-made pool cue that he always carried with him in his Dodge Durango. That conversation had lasted the length of her lunch, and when she'd finally given up on Noah, she'd agreed to play pool with him.

Josie wished she could have a do-over of this entire day. No, make it a do-over of the entire week. Her cat was still missing, and she wasn't any closer to finding Loretta's will. To make matters worse, Noah hadn't even come close to kissing her again.

She'd tried everything to entice him, but the man must be made of ice. She, on the other hand, had almost melted into the floor when she'd met him coming out of the shower last night, a towel slung low around his hips.

Of course, having Miles following her like a shadow around Noah's house hadn't helped. She'd tried every way she knew to gently encourage him to meet up with Doris and convince her to release Baby, but he'd kept putting Josie off with weak excuses. Josie couldn't tell whether Miles was afraid of Doris or just enjoying a break from her.

That's why she had to figure out her next move. She'd wanted to discuss it with Noah over lunch, but he'd stood her up. So, she'd finally agreed to let Vance buy her a beer and teach her the game of pool.

That way her day wouldn't be totally wasted.

He'd been a tenacious, hands-on instructor, but a few well-aimed jabs with her pool cue had taught him to keep a respectful distance. Now if she could only teach him to stop trying to seduce her.

"A pool stick is like a woman," he said, slowly

sliding one blunt-tipped finger down the length of his cue. "If you touch her just right, she'll do anything you want."

Josie tried not to gag on her beer. She set down the bottle on a nearby table. "It's your shot."

Vance leaned over the table, then shot three balls in quick succession, making each one. He grinned, his gaze roaming over the territory below her neck. "I can do it fast, or I can do it slow. Either way, I'm damn good."

His grin faded when he missed an easy bank shot.

He stared hard at the tip of his cue, as if baffled by its behavior. "Looks like I need some chalk."

She handed him the cube of blue chalk, then studied the table. "Only two balls left."

He chalked up his cue. "That's right, but they're awful tricky. If you sink the eight ball, then you win the game." His tone told her there was no chance of that happening.

She took her time studying the angles, then Josie leaned over the table to take aim.

Vance moved around the edge of the table until he was directly across from her, his gaze fixed on her cleavage. "You need to bend over just a little more, babe."

That did it. Time to teach Vance a lesson he'd never forget. At least this way her day wouldn't be a total loss.

She bent down until the tips of her breasts almost touched the table. "Is this better?"

He licked his lips. "Oh, honey, that's much better."

She took her aim, drew back her cue stick, then hesitated.

"What's wrong?"

She looked up at Vance. "What do I get if I make this shot?"

He gave her a slow smile. "Babe, I'll give you anything you want."

She pretended to think about it. "How about we bet twenty bucks?"

He laughed. "Hey, I don't want to take your money."

She chewed her lower lip. "But I really think I can make this one."

He shrugged his shoulders. "Okay, but it's tougher than it looks."

She pointed at the table with her cue stick. "Twenty bucks says I can sink it in that hole over there."

He gave her an indulgent smile. "It's called the corner pocket."

"Oh, that's right. I keep forgetting." She took careful aim once more, then executed her shot. The eight-ball bounced against the cushion three times, then rolled away from the pocket.

"Too bad," Vance said cheerfully. "It came mighty close."

She feigned a frown. "No do-overs?"

"No way." He grinned and held out his hand. "You owe me twenty bucks."

She retrieved her purse from the table and pulled out a twenty-dollar bill. "Well, if you won't let me shoot over, at least give me a chance to win my money back. Let's play another game, double or nothing."

He chuckled. "Honey, if you want to play with me, I'm not going to argue with you. Rack 'em up."

Noah strode into the Tenth Street Tavern. It took a moment for his eyes to adjust to the dim interior. In contrast to the hot, bright September afternoon, it was dark and cool inside. An elderly man sat in a booth near a large window, nursing a frosty mug of beer. The bald, middle-aged bartender stood at the bar, engrossed in a crossword puzzle. The whir of the ceiling fans hanging from the high ceiling blended with the honky-tonk music emanating from the corner jukebox.

The only other activity in the place was at the pool table located at the far end of the room. He heard a familiar laugh and his pulse quickened.

Josie.

He could hear her, but he couldn't see her due to the large man standing beside the pool table, blocking his view.

Relief at finding her here battled with irritation. Didn't she know that Doris might be following her? Didn't she know that the Tenth Street Tavern was no place for a woman alone? He moved toward her but stayed in the shadows until he finally caught sight of her. Then he stopped dead in his tracks.

She wore a sassy red halter dress that hugged her slender waist, flared out at her hips, and revealed much more of her cleavage than was necessary. Especially to the leering cretin playing pool with her.

"This is it," she said, unaware of Noah standing in the shadows. "Eight ball in the side pocket."

Her burly opponent wiped his brow. "You really are a fast learner."

She looked up and gave the man a brilliant smile. "That's because you're such a good teacher, Vance. I especially liked your lesson on how to *stroke it* just right."

Vance let the beer can slip from his grasp at the same moment she drew back her cue stick. The can clattered loudly on the tile floor, foamy beer spilling out of the top.

"Whoops." He gave her a sheepish smile. "Sorry."

She backed away from the table and chalked her cue. "No problem."

Noah watched Vance grab a towel from the bar, then kneel down on the floor and take his sweet time cleaning up the spilled beer.

"Hey, Josie," Vance said, still taking up room on the floor. "I forgot to tell you the story of how the town of Calamity got its name. You see, about one hundred and eighty years ago, there was a man who settled here by the name of Reid. Amos Reid. He was married and had nine beautiful daughters."

Noah folded his arms across his chest, recognizing a stall tactic when he saw one. The guy was trying to throw Josie off her game. But Josie didn't seem to mind. In fact, she perched herself on a stool and loosely held her pool cue in one hand.

"Nine daughters," she said. "That's a lot of girls."

Vance chuckled, digging the damp towel into every nook and cranny on the wooden floor. "Amos thought so, too. When his wife was with child again, he was certain his tenth child would be a boy. In fact, he boasted about it to everyone he saw."

Noah watched Vance begin to clean another spot on the floor.

"Amos was a natural leader among the settlers," Vance said, "and was revered for his even temperament. But when his tenth child was born, everyone within shouting distance could hear his howls of anger and disappointment."

Noah had heard this story several times growing up, but he had to admit Vance was a gifted storyteller. He glanced over at Josie, who was the picture of patience as she listened to Vance tell the tale.

"In fact," Vance said, "Amos was so upset about this development that he chose the name Calamity for his new infant daughter. Because she was the biggest calamity of his life."

"He sounds like a jerk," Josie mused.

Vance chuckled. "I'm sure he was, but nobody could change his mind about the name. Calamity's friends and family called her Callie, but her father *always* called her Calamity."

A slow smile spread over Vance's flushed face. "Until, one day, when Amos and all his daughters were out chopping weeds in a field. Folks back then often used a corn knife for that task, which is similar to a small machete. Anyway, before Amos knew what was happening, Calamity raced right to him and swung her corn knife only inches away from his chest."

"Wow." Josie's sank her upper teeth into her bottom lip.

"Amos screamed," Vance said, really getting into the story now. "He was certain his youngest daughter was trying to kill him. But then he saw the severed head of a rattlesnake fly through the air. You see, Calamity had seen that snake about to attack her father and chopped it off at the neck, saving his life."

"That's a great story."

"Oh, it gets better," Vance told her. "Amos was so grateful, he insisted that the town they were building be named after her. And that's how the town of Calamity got its name."

Josie applauded. "You're a wonderful storyteller, Vance." She hopped off the stool and approached the pool table. "In fact, I almost forgot it's my turn."

Vance cleared his throat. "It sure is. And there's a hundred bucks riding on this shot. Not to pressure you or anything."

She lined up her shot, then glanced up at him. "One hundred? I think you mean two hundred, don't you?"

He winced. "Oh, yeah, I guess you're right. Two hundred."

Noah watched in fascination as she focused her total concentration on the pool table. She took her shot, neatly pocketing the eight ball.

Vance sagged against the table. "Damn."

She replaced her cue stick on the rack, then walked over to him, holding out her hand. "It's been a pleasure playing pool with you this afternoon."

"You hustled me, girl," Vance grumbled under his breath as he pulled his wallet from his back pocket.

Josie smiled as she watched him place four fifty-dollar bills in her palm. "I guess some days you're the corn knife, and other days you're the snake."

"I guess so," he said grudgingly. He grabbed his beer and pool cue before heading to the bar.

Josie tapped the bills together, then turned around, her face paling the instant she saw Noah. "What are you doing here?"

"You invited me for lunch, remember?" He looked pointedly at the money in her hands. "The question is, where the hell did you learn to play pool like that?" She shrugged her shoulders, not quite meeting his gaze. "I just got lucky."

"And made a tidy chunk of change. But I don't think it was luck."

Her cheeks flushed and she turned slightly away from him. "This helps make up for the cost of my tire repair." She opened her purse and stuffed the money inside.

Vance walked up to them, a fresh beer in his hand and a fierce scowl on his face. "Is this guy bothering you, Josie?"

"No. I'm fine, Vance. Really."

Vance turned to Noah and stuck out his jaw. "All the same, I think you should walk away from the lady."

Noah smiled at his tough guy act. "You're joking, right?"

Vance took a menacing step closer to him. "Do I look like I'm joking?"

Josie quickly stepped between them. "I'll vouch for him, Vance. This is Noah Tanner. He is my boyfriend."

"Noah Tanner?" Vance looked him up and down. "Hey, you're that guy Amber McNair dumped to marry Shawn Henderson."

"That's right," Noah admitted, wondering if every stranger in town knew his business.

Vance grinned, then held out one hand. "I'm Vance McNair, Amber's second cousin. We missed you at the wedding ceremony."

"Something came up," Noah said, reaching out to shake his hand. "But I made it to the reception." This was just another reason a man shouldn't rush into marriage, he told himself. Who knew what kind of unsavory relatives might pop out of the woodwork.

"Something came up?" Vance shook his head. "That's lame. Weren't you supposed to be the best man?"

"It's a long story," Noah clipped.

The bartender leaned across the bar and shouted, "Hey, Vance, your order's up."

After he left, Noah escorted Josie to the nearest

table. "Something tells me you'd heard that Calamity story before."

"Yes, from Loretta," Josie said with a reminiscent smile. "She loved it! Calamity Reid was one of her ancestors. Loretta even kept her maiden name when she married because she was so proud of her heritage. And she wanted me to have a piece of it, too."

"So, what are you doing in this run-down joint?" He sat down across from her. "Other than getting lucky at pool."

"I thought if I started going out in public more, it might draw out Doris. But she didn't show."

"Draw out Doris? Are you crazy?"

"I'm just tired of wasting time." She closed her eyes. "I miss my cat. And I need to honor Loretta's wishes by finding her new will and getting it to her lawyer. I have a dream job waiting for me in San Antonio, but my life's been on hold ever since I arrived here. And that *is* driving me crazy."

"I get it," he said. "But what else can you do?"

"I don't know," she said with a determined gleam in her eye. "But I need to think of something."

Chapter Fifteen

That evening, Josie knew what she had to do. She'd been keeping her life a secret for too long. Noah had watched her hustle a man at pool earlier that day. He'd seen her hot-wire a car and jimmy door locks with a paper clip. He needed to know the truth about her, because she wasn't just pretending to be in love with him anymore. When she'd seen him standing in that tavern, she knew for certain.

Josie was falling in love with him. And falling hard.

That could be a problem. Because she knew from painful experience that if she didn't reveal her true self, it would eventually come out. Usually in the worst way possible.

The truth *always* came out.

"It's your bet." Noah sat at the kitchen table, slowly fanning open the playing cards in his hand.

A sultry breeze sifted through the open windows and a chorus of crickets welcomed the full moon. Miles had offered to close up the coffee shop this evening to give Noah a break. So, it was just the two of them.

Josie stared at her cards as the ceiling fan whirred above her.

"Is something wrong?" Noah asked her. "You've hardly said a word since we left the tavern."

She lowered her cards and cleared her throat. "I'm fine."

"You're disappointed," he said. "Because we're no closer to getting your cat back than we were yesterday. That's it, isn't it?"

She licked her lips, feeling guilty because for the past few hours her mind hadn't been on her cat at all. Or even on finding Loretta's will. Just more proof that she probably deserved her fate.

"Don't give up. Maybe Doris will accept money instead of the will. I've got five thousand in savings I can loan you. Then you can get your cat back."

She blinked at him. "Five thousand dollars?"

"Look, I probably should have offered you the money in the first place." He looked sheepish. "I just thought it would be resolved by now. If anything happens to your cat..."

She swallowed hard. “I can’t take your money, Noah.”

“I want to help you, Josie. These last few days have been…” His voice trailed off, then he said, “It’s just that I’ve never met a woman like you before.”

That was an understatement. She squared her shoulders. This was the moment to tell him everything. To lay her cards on the table—figuratively and literally.

She could start at the beginning.

She could tell him how she’d been abandoned at a fire station as an infant, just hours after her birth. How the name Josie had been taped to her blanket, but there was no last name and no way to contact her birth parents. How she was put into the foster care system while different state agencies spent years searching for her parents or any other blood relatives.

By the time they gave up, she was past the prime age range for adoption. Then she bounced from foster home to foster home, never quite fitting in anywhere. Never finding a family she could call her own.

Or maybe she could tell Noah about her dreams.

She wanted the white picket fence and the swing set in the backyard. A tree house for her kids to play in with their friends. She wanted a job that kept her fulfilled and challenged. Most of all, she wanted someone special to share her life with. A father for her children. A lover who fulfilled all her fantasies.

She wanted *him*.

Josie cleared her throat. "You don't really know me, Noah."

He smiled at her—that boyish smile that always made her heart skip a beat.

"I know you can be stubborn," he said. "And that you're smart. Beautiful. Sexy." His gaze softened on her. "And I know I can't resist you anymore."

Her heart flipped over in her chest. She dropped her gaze to her cards and took a deep, steadying breath. "Is it my bet?"

He studied her for a moment, then leaned back in his chair. "I just raised you two toothpicks."

"Oh." She stared at her cards, not really seeing them. Something had changed between them. Noah had let down his guard. He *trusted* her.

Turmoil roiled inside of her. It would be so easy to keep her secrets. To keep her past behind her, where it belonged. But it wouldn't be honest. Or fair to him. Especially since he'd done so much to help her from the very first moment they'd met. She owed him more than gratitude.

She owed him the truth.

"The secret of this game is the bluff," he said, misinterpreting her silence. "You don't want to give away the strength or weakness of your hand to your opponent. That way I won't know whether you're risking ten toothpicks on a royal flush or a pair of deuces."

She glanced down at the table. "I only have one toothpick left."

"Then you'll have to bet something else." A mischievous twinkle lit his brown eyes. "I know. Ever play strip poker?"

Josie opened her mouth, then closed it again. If she wasn't brave enough to tell him the naked truth, maybe she could show him. "Okay, you're on."

An hour later, their strip poker game had led to Josie losing two earrings and a shoe. Noah had lost his cowboy boots, his socks, his watch, his shirt, and his belt. Now he was down to his denim blue jeans, and he didn't look happy about it.

"This isn't as much fun as I thought it would be," he grumbled.

Her gaze centered on his bare broad chest. "I'm having a great time."

Noah shook his head. "I've heard of beginner's luck, but this is ridiculous. You've won almost every hand."

"It's your bet," she reminded him.

He looked at the cards in his hand, then rubbed one finger over his square chin. "I'm afraid your luck has just run out, Josie. I'll see your shoe and raise my pants."

She smiled. "Now there's an intriguing picture. I'll go ahead and call your bet."

He frowned. "Are you sure you want to do that?"

"Positive."

He laid his cards on the table. "I've got a pair of aces."

"Good hand." She fanned her cards out in front of him. "Only not good enough. I have three queens." She leaned back in her chair. "Take off your pants."

"Where have I heard that before?" He rose to his feet.

Josie's mouth went dry as his broad hands moved to the waistband of his jeans. She should stop him now. Tell him he'd never stood a chance in the first place. Unfortunately, she'd never been good at resisting temptation.

She cupped her chin in her hand. "Will I see Mickey Mouse again?"

He unzipped his jeans. "Something much better. And hotter."

"Be still my heart." Only she wasn't joking. Her heart was beating an erratic tattoo in her chest, and she couldn't quite catch her breath.

Noah shoved his jeans to his ankles, then stepped out of them. No Mickey Mouse this time. Instead, he wore a pair of light-blue boxer shorts imprinted with race cars.

She'd done it. She'd stripped him naked. Well, almost naked.

"Now it's your turn," he said, echoing her thoughts as he moved toward her.

She rose unsteadily to her feet. "Noah, I..."

He caught her and kissed her before she could say another word. His strong arms wrapped around her, pulling her close enough to feel the warmth of his skin. Her fingers splayed over his bare back as his mouth devoured her own.

She closed her eyes, growing dizzy with the kiss and the lack of air and the knowledge that Noah wanted her. *Really* wanted her. There was nothing fake about him.

His fingers threaded through her hair, then cupped her face as he abandoned her mouth to scatter kisses over her nose and forehead and chin.

"I've wanted to do this for so long," he breathed against her neck. "It almost seems like forever."

"I know," she murmured, leaning into him. "I know."

He pulled back just far enough to trace the soft curve of her cheek. "You're perfect."

She stiffened, then backed out of his arms. "You're wrong, Noah. I'm not perfect. I'm far from perfect."

He tilted his head in confusion. "Why would you say that?"

She took a deep breath, the pain of the truth cutting into her like a knife. "Well, for starters, I know how to bluff. In fact, I've been doing it all week."

His brows drew together. "Doing what?"

"Bluffing. About everything." She gave a small shrug. "Well, almost everything."

The coolness she felt in the room wasn't coming from the open windows. Noah stared at her for a long, uncomfortable moment. "Such as?"

She forced herself to meet his penetrating gaze. "How do you feel about the fact that I used to be a pool hustler for a living?"

He blinked. "What?"

"And poker. Did you know you have a 'tell'? Whenever you're bluffing, you rub your chin. I've become quite good at spotting tells over the years, although hustling pool was where I made the most money."

"Like at the Tenth Street Tavern?"

She nodded. "Vance made a perfect pigeon. Cocky and overconfident. Easy pickings."

"Just like me," he murmured, more to himself than to her.

She motioned helplessly toward the table. "Tonight was just for fun."

"Fun," he echoed flatly. He glanced down at his boxer shorts. "Guess I turned out to be easy pickings, too."

She could feel him slipping away from her. "Please, let me explain."

"I think I've already heard enough. Let me keep a few illusions."

But she wouldn't let him walk away without telling him everything. "You told me about your childhood and how tough it was. How your parents weren't really there for you. Well, the same was true for me. Except, I never knew my parents. They gave me away right after I was born. I don't even know their names. Or what they look like. Or why they couldn't keep me."

He stared at her, not saying a word.

"It was rough," she admitted. "I had to find a way to survive, whether it was in a new foster home or on the streets. That's where I learned things like counting cards, pool hustling, hot-wiring cars, and how to jimmy a lock. For a while, during my teenage years, those things helped keep me alive, because I didn't have anyone who cared about me."

"Josie, I..."

She held up one hand, afraid she wouldn't be able to finish her story if she stopped now. "It's nobody's fault, really. And it didn't take me long to realize that kind of life wasn't sustainable. I somehow still managed to attend school and actually thrived there. I earned scholarships to college and was determined to make something of myself. To find my own value."

"And you did," he said in a husky whisper.

But she still wasn't finished. "Do you know why majoring in history mattered to me so much? Because I have no family history of my own. None. It's just a blank page in my past."

Josie knew she was talking too fast, but she needed to get it all out, certain she would never have another chance.

"And I had no ties to anyone," she said, "until I met Loretta Reid. She became my family, and so did Baby. That's why I was so desperate to save my cat the day we met and why I have to keep my promise to Loretta, even it means missing out on that job in San Antonio."

The muscle at his jaw ticked.

Josie's voice cracked, and she sucked in a deep breath, determined to finish. "I should have told you the truth sooner." She looked around the house. "The game we've been playing to make people believe we're a couple started fooling me, too." She rose to her feet. "But don't worry, Noah. I know I don't belong here."

Noah took a step toward her, then the front door opened, and Miles walked in.

Miles blanched at the sight of Noah wearing only his boxer shorts. "What the hell is going on here?"

"Nothing," Noah said, turning toward him. "Why aren't you at the coffee shop?"

Miles crossed his arms. "Because I thought I should tell you about the fire in person."

"Fire?" Noah moved toward him, his body tense. "What fire?"

"The one at Blue Moon," Miles said. "But don't panic. I called the fire department right away and they did a fantastic job of getting the flames under control." His brow furrowed, as if he was deep in thought. "Do you think I'm too old to become a firefighter?"

"You should have called me!" Noah swept up his blue jeans from the floor and hastily stepped into them.

Miles stuck out his chin. "You left me specific instructions not to bother you tonight. I wasn't even supposed to be covering the evening shift for you, remember? But you insisted."

"Save the excuses, Miles." Noah pulled his black T-shirt over his head. "Just tell me what happened. Was anyone hurt?"

"No. It was almost closing time when the fire started."

"How did it start?" Josie clutched the back of the

chair, desperately hoping the coffee shop hadn't sustained too much damage. "Please tell us, Miles."

Miles sighed. "The firemen said it was probably a wiring defect in the cappuccino machine. The cord burst into flames, so I immediately called 9-1-1."

"That's it?" Noah glared at him. "Just the cord?"

"And a stack of coffee filters," Miles said. "There might have been some napkins scorched, too. And part of a wall. It was a very traumatic event. It's all kind of blurry."

Noah didn't say a word as he pulled on his cowboy boots. "I'd better run down there and take a look for myself. And I'll need to call Shelby and Taylor to tell them what happened."

"Do you want me to come with you?" Josie asked him.

"No, there's no reason for us both to go." Noah met her gaze. "But let's talk when I get back."

She nodded, then watched him head out the door.

As soon as it closed behind him, Miles hurried to her side. "We don't have much time. Doris was with me at Blue Moon when the fire happened. I had invited her there to talk about our marriage. Now she's waiting for me at our favorite diner so we can continue the conversation."

"I don't understand," Josie said, confused.

Miles put his hands on her shoulders and gave

them a light shake. "This is the perfect time for you to get your cat. I circled by the house after leaving Blue Moon to unlock the front door for you. And I'll keep Doris away from the house as long as I can, but you must hurry! She's still pretty angry with me."

Josie just stood there for a moment, letting his words sink in. "I can save Baby?"

"Yes but do it fast. I don't know how long I can stall her."

"Thank you, Miles," Josie said before racing out into the night.

Chapter Sixteen

Josie drove down the street as the moon lit her path to the historic district. Lamplight glowed in the windows of the snug houses lining the neighborhood. She'd wanted to live in a place like this so badly when she was growing up. There had been a few foster homes in similar neighborhoods. She'd even spent a month in a beautiful brick home that seemed like a castle.

But for some reason, her stay with those families never lasted very long.

It was usually no one's fault. A job transfer to another state. A divorce. An unexpected death. Many of her foster parents had felt badly about sending her back into the system, but they'd had to put their own families first.

She understood that now, but at the time it just seemed like another abandonment. The silver lining to that string of disappointments was learning that she needed to forge her own path if she wanted her life to change.

As her Mazda Miata rounded a corner, the headlights illuminated another house—the beautiful Victorian home where Loretta had grown up and where the Dooleys now squatted. She slowly pulled along the curb, then shifted into Park, letting the car idle. The house was completely dark and there was no vehicle in the driveway or the carport.

Miles hadn't steered her wrong.

She parked along the street in front of the house, then quickly got out of her car. There was no time to waste. Her pulse quickened as she walked purposefully toward the front door. This had gone on long enough. She was going to rescue Baby tonight, no matter what it took. Finding Loretta's new will and testament would have to wait—there wasn't enough time for a more thorough search of the house.

Josie wondered what Noah would think if he could see her right now. No matter how much she tried to improve her life, she'd never be able to mold herself into some cookie-cutter design of the perfect woman. Such a creature didn't exist. And she had no desire to be perfect.

She walked through the front door, then closed it quietly behind her. A table lamp illuminated enough of the room to assure her that it was empty. The old house was completely silent. Moving into the hallway, she hurried toward the door that led to the basement.

With one last look over her shoulder, she started walking down the stairs.

* * *

"Hey, Tanner, sounds like you had a little excitement here tonight."

Noah looked up from the counter to see Deputy Trey Booker framed in the doorway of the Blue Moon Coffee Shop. "How did you hear about it?"

"The call came over on the police scanner. I just wanted to stop and check out the damage. You know I won't be able to live without my morning espresso and biscotti."

"Your breakfast will be waiting for you tomorrow, just like always." He held up a fried electrical cord. "Unfortunately, the cappuccino machine bit the dust. Faulty wiring."

Trey leaned over the coffee counter and peered at the charred drywall. "Looks like you might want to file a claim with your insurance company."

"Thanks for the advice," Noah said dryly. He looked up to see Miles walk into the coffee shop, stopping short when he spotted the uniformed deputy.

"Hey, Deputy Booker," Miles called out, waving one hand in the air. "I just want you to know I'm innocent. I had nothing to do with starting that fire."

"Relax, Miles," the deputy said. "I'm not here to arrest you."

"Oh." Miles visibly relaxed. "Good."

Noah turned to Miles. "I thought you were going to stay at the ranch."

"I decided to come back here and see if you needed help with cleanup."

"I appreciate that," Noah said, somewhat surprised by the gesture. "But we can take care of most of it tomorrow. Although my guess is that we'll stay pretty busy just answering customer questions about the fire."

"Then maybe I should sharpen my storytelling skills." Miles cleared his throat. "It was the best of cappuccino machines; it was the worst of cappuccino machines..."

Noah quickly ushered him out the door, telling Miles he needed a good night's sleep after all the excitement.

Noah waited until Miles left the shop before he turned back to the deputy. "I suppose I should mention that I suspect the fire might have been started intentionally."

Booker arched a brow. "By whom?"

Noah shrugged. "Miles came to mind, but despite his... idiosyncrasies, I don't believe he's a violent person. Not intentionally, anyway."

"Who else then?"

"His wife, Doris Dooley. She was here earlier this evening having coffee with Miles."

Booker looked thoughtful. "You know, after the last time we talked, I decided to do a little research on your friend Doris."

"Did you find anything interesting?"

"Not really. There were a couple of neighbor complaints about too much noise coming from the Dooley residence. Apparently, Miles and Doris like to yell a lot—especially at each other."

"Anything else?" Noah asked.

"Nothing criminal if that's what you're thinking. When I asked around the office about the Dooleys, one of the deputies mentioned that Doris had badgered him to dance with her at a neighborhood party. He said she was very insistent."

Noah shifted uncomfortably on his feet, remembering how Doris had harassed him right out of his clothes. "I wonder how many other people she's badgered that haven't come forward."

"Hard to say. But no one has filed a complaint about her."

"Josie has a legitimate complaint," Noah told him. "Doris still has her cat."

"Before you start flinging accusations, answer a few questions for me." The deputy folded his thick arms across his chest. "Did you enter the Dooley house under false pretenses? Did you take off your pants in front of Doris? How was Josie involved?"

Noah opened his mouth, then closed it again. He wasn't about to squeal on Josie for breaking and entering. No matter how much she'd screwed up his life. He was still reeling from her revelations this evening. He hated secrets. He hated lies even more. But she hadn't technically lied to him. He'd just never bothered to ask Josie about her past.

Great, he was rationalizing now. That was a bad sign.

"I'm still waiting." Booker cleared his throat.

"I'm pleading the fifth."

"I thought so." Booker leveled his perceptive gaze on him. "Look, I realize Doris Dooley has probably made your lives hell, but until I have solid proof, I can't do anything about it. Otherwise, it's just your word against hers, and you two aren't exactly squeaky-clean, either."

"What kind of proof do you need?"

A wry smile tipped up one corner of Trey's mouth. "A written confession would be nice."

"Fat chance. But you might want to contact a woman by the name of Louisa Murillo who works at the town morgue. She's an old friend of Miles' and might have more information about the couple."

"Thanks," the deputy said. "I'll do that."

"Is there anything you want me to do?"

The deputy flipped his notepad closed. "As a matter of fact, there is. Try to keep yourself and Josie out of trouble. It sounds like you've both crossed the line a time or two already."

Noah nodded, then looked up at his friend. "How did you know you were in love with Mina?"

Trey's dark brows rose up to his hairline. "Where did *that* come from?"

"It's just a simple question."

"Well, let's see, the first time I met Mina..."

"I was there with you," Noah said, "so you can skip the preliminaries. In fact, I'm the one who introduced you to her, remember?"

Trey laughed. "I remember she turned you down flat when you tried one of your lame pickup lines on her."

Noah shrugged. "I was just trying to make you look good."

"Well, you succeeded. To this day, she still thanks me for rescuing her."

"Very funny," Noah quipped. "Seriously, though, when did you know?"

Trey sat on a stool. "It would have to be the night she got sick in my car."

Noah blanched. "Not your classic Maserati?"

"The very one. We'd been out to a new restaurant downtown. On the way home I found out that Mediterranean food does not agree with her."

"Your black Maserati with the turbo engine?" Noah asked, just for clarification.

"One and the same." Trey breathed a long sigh. "But it was the moment I knew for sure."

"Knew what?"

His dark eyes softened. "That I'd fallen in love with her."

Noah looked around the empty coffee shop, then back at the detective. "Am I missing something here?"

"Don't you get it, Tanner? I was more worried about Mina than my car."

"But you love that car."

"Exactly. Only I love Mina a hell of a lot more." He glanced at his watch, then rose off the bar stool.

"Speaking of which, I should have been home twenty minutes ago."

Noah locked the door after him, then did a quick walk-through of the coffee shop, just to make certain everything was back in order before he headed home.

* * *

Noah found Miles waiting for him at the ranch.

"What's the total damage?" Miles asked as soon as Noah walked into the house.

"Most of it was cosmetic," Noah said, answering Miles' question. "And the property insurance should cover all of it."

"Well, that's good to hear. It sounds like it could have been a lot worse if that fire had spread."

"It didn't, thanks to your quick action." Noah saw an empty coffee cup on an end table. It was Josie's favorite cup. "I didn't see Josie's car in the driveway. Did she go somewhere?"

Miles shrugged. "I heard her leave, but I figured she was going to join you at the Blue Moon. I'm not sure where she is."

Noah didn't know whether to be disappointed or relieved. On the one hand, he wanted time to think over everything she'd told him. On the other hand, he was itching to see her again. Touch her again. And most important of all, kiss her again.

But it was late, and he was exhausted. If he tried to stay up and wait for her to return, he'd be asleep on the leather sofa within the next five minutes. Better to go upstairs to his room and get a good night's sleep. Tomorrow morning would be soon enough to tell Josie exactly how he felt about her.

Josie crept slowly down basement staircase, feeling her way along the wooden railing in the darkness. It was cooler here and smelled slightly damp. When she reached the landing, she moved her hand along the old brick wall, searching for a light switch. She encountered dust and several cobwebs before she finally located it.

She flipped on the switch and two light bulbs illuminated the cluttered basement. Crates and boxes lined the old plaster walls, and a pink feather boa hung haphazardly out of one of them. An old makeup mirror stood in one corner, next to a naked, headless mannequin. Sections of scenery and stage props lay scattered across the floor.

It looked like Miles had done more than volunteer at the theater. He'd actually brought bits and pieces of it home with him. The dank, dusty air invaded her nostrils, making her sneeze.

Then she heard a plaintive meow.

"Baby?" She hurried across the basement, tripping over a broken piano stool. She hit the rough cement floor, scraping her knees. But the angle allowed her to see Baby. The gray cat stood watching her, partially hidden in the open space between the foundation wall and the first floor.

Josie stood up and rushed forward. Baby leaped into her arms, mewing and rubbing her furry head against Josie's neck. Tears stung her eyes as she hugged her cat close. A moment later, she heard a familiar purr emanating from Baby's furry chest.

"How are you?" Josie whispered, stroking the cat's head and scratching behind her ears. Baby closed her eyes in deep contentment. Despite the cat's captivity, she actually seemed to have gained some weight. No doubt that was due to the wide-open bag of cat food in the basement that gave her an endless supply of nutrition.

Then Josie noticed a small dish full of anchovies sitting on a fancy cat tower, along with a pet activity center that looked brand new. "Wow, Baby, you've been living in luxury. I hope you're not going to turn into one of those spoiled fat cats."

There was also a water bowl filled with fresh water

and the litter box was surprisingly clean, all leading Josie to believe her beloved cat hadn't suffered much during her captivity.

But it was time to go home.

Standing up, she cradled Baby in her arms. "We're getting out of here."

The cat began to purr, nestling her head against Josie's collarbone. Tears of joy and relief filled her eyes as she hurried toward the stairs. She'd suppressed her fears for so long, and now they threatened to burst forth. Josie had lost Baby, then found her again. And tonight, she might have lost Noah—possibly forever.

"Be very quiet now," Josie instructed Baby as she carefully climbed up the steep staircase. She winced at each creak along the way.

Josie was almost at the top of the stairs when she heard a sound that made her freeze in place. Dread filled her as the sound grew louder. She gently set Baby down and shooed her back toward her hiding place in the basement.

The sirens were deafening now, and Josie knew there was no escape.

Chapter Seventeen

The next morning, Noah walked into the kitchen and found the last person he expected to see sitting at his kitchen table. "Shawn? How the hell did you get in here?"

His best friend looked up from his bowl of cereal. "I still have the key to your house that you gave me when we were ten years old. Remember?"

"Oh, yeah. That's right."

Shawn picked up a glass of orange juice. "I'm checking up on you, Noah. Why haven't you called me?"

Noah grabbed a glass out of the cupboard, then pulled out a chair and sat down at the table. "I thought you were still on your honeymoon. So why would I call you?"

"Oh, I don't know. Maybe because Blue Moon almost burned to the ground last night."

"That's a wild exaggeration." Noah reached for the carton of orange juice, then filled his glass to the brim. "There was some slight damage due to a faulty electrical cord. How did you hear about it?"

"Amber and I received a police scanner for a wedding present. We've been listening to it every night."

"Well, that sounds romantic," Noah quipped, not bothering to hide his sarcasm. It was a little early in the morning for him to have unexpected visitors.

"So, tell me more about this fire." Shawn leaned back in his chair. "How did it start? Do Shelby and Taylor know about it?"

"I sent them a text last night, along with some photos. They'll be contacting their insurance provider this morning, but they're not cutting their trip short."

"Well, that's good news, I guess."

"The fire damage was limited," Noah said. "Faulty wiring, a little smoke, minimal damage. The customers won't even notice."

Shawn looked surprised. "So, you're planning to open today?"

"Of course. Do you think I'd just be sitting here if there was considerable damage? I'd be out getting estimates, filing claims, and hiring contractors."

Shawn held up one hand. "Take it easy. Jeez, you always were cranky in the morning. Makes me feel sorry for Josie." He leaned forward, a devilish smile on his face. "So have you two set a wedding date yet?"

Noah stared at him. "What the hell are you talking about?"

"You've heard of a wedding, right? Flowers, tuxedoes, hives. Ring a bell?"

Noah shook his head, thoroughly confused. "What makes you think I'm getting married?"

"Because I've known you long enough that I can read you like a book. You're crazy about that girl. I could see it the night of the wedding reception. Besides, the word around town is that she's been living on the ranch with you."

Noah downed the rest of his juice. "I can't control the gossips around here."

Miles stumbled into the kitchen, then blinked at Shawn. "What's going on?"

"We're eating breakfast," Shawn said, helping himself to more juice. "You're welcome to join us."

Miles ignored him and turned to Noah. "What have you done with Josie?"

"What do you mean?" A prickle of apprehension crawled up Noah's spine. "I haven't seen her yet this morning."

"Neither have I." Miles began to pace. "But she's

not in her bed."

Noah glowered at him. "What were you doing in her bedroom?"

"I wanted to return a book I borrowed from her. But she's gone."

Noah pushed out his chair. "Gone where? Is her car outside?"

"No, it's not. And she's not upstairs or anywhere else in the house. I've already looked. "Did you say something to scare her off?"

"Of course not." It suddenly hit him that she might have misinterpreted his silence. Naturally, he'd been surprised by her revelation. And his pride might have been a little bruised when she'd bested him at poker. Not to mention the fact that he'd been standing there in his boxer shorts while she was still fully dressed.

His gut twisted as another thought occurred to him. A possibility he didn't even want to consider. Without another word, Noah bolted out of his chair and headed for the staircase. He could hear Miles and Shawn following behind him. Taking the steps two at a time, he rounded the wooden newel post at the top of the stairs and knocked sharply on her bedroom door.

"I already told you," Miles said from behind him. "She's not in there."

Noah swung open the door and strode into the

room. Miles was right—it was empty. He went over to the neatly made bed and pulled down the covers. The sheets were cold to the touch.

But that wasn't his only clue that she hadn't slept here. The freshly laundered sheets were smooth, with not one wrinkle or crease. The crisp white pillowcase didn't have one strand of silky blond hair on it. All of which made him suspect the worst—Josie had left the house last night.

And she'd never come back.

* * *

Less than an hour later, Noah tracked down Trey Booker at the sheriff's office. "She's gone."

Trey looked up from his desk. "Who's gone?"

"Josie. She's missing." Noah started to pace. His heart hadn't stopped pounding since he'd left the house. Guilt tore at him when he thought about Josie being in danger. All while he'd slept peacefully in his bed. "I think Doris is involved. Hell, I can't think of any other explanation."

"Calm down."

Noah raked one hand through his hair. "Don't tell me to calm down! *Josie is missing*. I think she's been missing for the past twelve hours. What if..." He stopped, unable to put his worst fears into words.

"She's not missing."

Noah stared stupidly at him. "What?"

"I said she's not missing." Trey rose to his feet. "Josie is here. She was arrested last night."

He stared at Trey in disbelief. "Arrested?"

"Yes, for unlawful entry," Trey explained.

Noah sagged down into a chair. "There must be some mistake."

"She was caught in the act this time," Trey said. "Sorry, buddy. I know that's not what you want to hear."

He couldn't believe it. But until recently, he never would have believed she was a pool hustler. Or that she could so easily beat the pants off him in poker. What other secrets was Josie Reid hiding from him?

He mentally shook himself. This was crazy. Only one explanation made sense. He leveled his gaze on Trey. "Doris Dooley is behind all this, isn't she?"

The deputy flipped open the file on his desk. "Mrs. Dooley reported the incident at 11:47 last night. She prevented Josie from leaving her house until a cruiser arrived to pick her up."

Noah raked a hand through his hair. "I'm sure she was there just to get her cat."

"The officer didn't see a cat, but he did report hearing a cat meowing from the basement. Mrs. Dooley told him the cat belonged to her."

"But that's a lie," Noah said between clenched teeth.

"Josie freely admitted to entering the Dooley home," Trey said. "However, she claims Miles Dooley not only gave her permission to enter the house, but also told her he left the front door unlocked."

"See! I told you."

"I called a few minutes before you got here. He denies that ever happened."

"This doesn't make any sense at all," he said, rising out of the chair. "Let me see Josie. Then we can straighten this whole mess out."

"Hold it, Noah." Trey held up one hand. "You can't see her."

"Why the hell not?"

"Because she specifically requested *not* to see you. But don't worry, she has a lawyer."

"She doesn't need a lawyer! Don't you get it, Trey? This is all a setup. You can't hold Josie on the basis of these ridiculous charges."

"She's got a bail hearing scheduled in three hours." Trey sat forward in his chair. "If you want to get her out of here, I suggest you bring your checkbook." Trey's tone softened. "Look, Noah, I'm on your side. But my hands are tied. Josie was caught entering the Dooley house unlawfully."

"There's got to be something more we can do."

Trey shook his head. "I'm really sorry, but it's too late. The only thing that will stop the process now is if Doris Dooley drops the charges. And after all we've learned about her, what do you think the chances are of that happening?"

Noah headed for the door. "Maybe better than you think."

* * *

Deputy Trey Booker escorted Josie to a special holding room. When they reached the door, he turned to her. "I'll give you ten minutes. I'm already bending the rules by allowing this visit."

"Thank you, Deputy," she said as Trey opened the door for her.

"Josie!" Miles jumped to his feet and rushed over to her. He took her hands in his, then stepped back a pace, his horrified gaze raking over her. "I'm so sorry. I had no idea Doris would be there." He shook his head. "You look awful."

"I'm fine, really. But you'd better sit down. You look a little pale."

Miles took her advice but pulled out a chair for her first. "I couldn't believe it when I heard you were in jail. I mean, why didn't you call us last night and tell us what happened?"

"I'm used to handling things myself." The events of the previous night still seemed more like a nightmare than a reality. The flashing red police lights outside Loretta's historic home. The officer reading her Miranda rights. The endless, exhausting questions.

"Noah was pretty mad about it," Miles told her.

"I can imagine," she said dryly. At least she'd been spared the humiliation of Noah witnessing her arrest.

"I'm much more understanding." Miles scooted his chair closer to her. "I know somebody incarcerated at a minimum-security prison near here. She was Mom's cellmate."

She blinked at him in surprise. "I had no idea your mom was in prison."

He shrugged. "It's a long story and we've got much more important things to discuss."

"We do?"

"Yes, like your bail money. I know a bail bondsman who provides services pretty cheap. He might even give us a special rate."

"I really appreciate that, but..."

"Just listen," Miles said. "In return, all you have to do is promise to marry me."

She blinked. "What?"

He gazed at her with his soulful eyes. "I'm not sure things are going to work out between me and Doris. That's why I like to have a backup plan. You and I could have a long engagement to give both of us enough time to get used to the idea. I'll write you often and show up on visiting days."

"Oh, Miles," Josie began, wondering if this was some crazy nightmare. "That's very sweet. But that wouldn't be fair to you."

"I don't mind waiting for you."

"That's not what I mean," she said gently. "I don't love you."

"Oh, that doesn't matter. I'm sure it would make Aunt Loretta very happy to know her two favorite people in the world were together. And this way we can share her inheritance."

Josie's smile faded as she suddenly realized what his surprising proposal was all about. "Well, the first problem is you're already married. But even more importantly, I'm in love with someone else."

His face fell. "You mean Noah?"

"I'm afraid so."

He sighed. "I had a feeling there was something going on between the two of you when I saw him in his boxer shorts."

Someone knocked on the door, then Deputy Booker stuck his head inside. "Time's up."

Miles turned to her. "I'll still call the bail bondsman for you. And I'll make him give you the special rate, too."

"Thank you, Miles," she said, ready for this nightmare to end.

After Miles left, Deputy Booker turned to her. "You may not need bail money."

She looked up at him. "What do you mean?"

"Well, I probably shouldn't be telling you this, but Noah was here earlier. In fact, he almost punched me when I said he couldn't see you."

Despite her situation, a tiny flicker of hope lit inside of her. "He was here?"

Trey nodded, then grinned. "That boy has got it bad."

She frowned in confusion. "Are we talking about the same Noah Tanner? The one who likes fast trucks and temporary women?"

"That's the one."

She swallowed hard. "I've changed my mind, Deputy. I would like to see him."

"Too late. He already left."

"Oh." Disappointment wafted through her. "Do you know where he's going?"

"From the way he talked, I'd say he's headed for Doris Dooley's place."

Josie shot out of her chair. "You've got to stop him. Please, before she frames him, too."

Deputy Booker arched a brow. "You were framed?"

"It's a long story, but the short answer is yes. If you leave right now, you might still be able to catch him."

"Noah Tanner knows how to take care of himself. You, however, seem to attract trouble like a magnet." Trey pulled a chair toward him, then straddled the back of it. "Now, I'm not going anywhere until you tell me everything, Ms. Reid. Why don't you start at the very beginning."

Chapter Eighteen

Doris Dooley opened the front door of her house and greeted her guest with a wide smile. She wore black stretch jeans and an orange Longhorn sweatshirt that matched the orange polish on her fingernails.

"Well, look who it is! Wade Calhoun stopping by to sell me insurance again. You sure are persistent."

"Good morning, Doris," Noah said politely. "May I come in?"

"Of course." She stepped back a pace and motioned him inside. "I thought you'd never get here."

"I didn't know you were expecting me," he said, walking into her living room.

"Somehow, I just got the feeling you'd show up this morning. In fact, I was banking on it, if you know what I mean."

"I think I do." He looked around the cluttered

living room, noting the dirty ashtray on the coffee table next to an issue of *Variety* and a vintage cordless phone. They'd turned this beautiful home into a cluttered mess in just a few short weeks. He wouldn't call them hoarders, but they were definitely headed in that direction.

Noah turned to face Doris. "I'm here about Josie."

"Big surprise," she quipped, closing the door behind him. "You've shown quite an interest in her. Or are you more interested in the money she might inherit from Aunt Loretta's estate?"

"I don't care about Loretta Reid's estate. And neither does Josie; she's just trying to honor her last wishes."

"Sure, she is," Doris said. "Miles is Loretta's only kin. He's just trying to honor her last wishes too."

"That's for a probate court to figure out. So, let's stop playing games." He took a step closer to her. "I'm asking you to drop the charges against Josie."

Doris tugged a raven curl behind her ear. "Why in the world would I do that?"

Noah pulled a folded cashier's check out of his shirt pocket. "Here are one thousand reasons."

Her eyes widened in surprise. "Wow, that's not what I was expecting." She reached for the check, but he slipped it back into his pocket. "You have to earn it first."

She fluttered her eyelashes at him, thick with heavy black mascara. "What exactly did you have in mind?"

He picked up the cordless phone. "Call Deputy Trey Booker and tell him you made a big mistake. That you'd like to drop the charges against Josie."

Doris shook her head, her face growing pale. "Miles would be furious with me."

That's when it clicked. Realization washed over him like a tidal wave, almost knocking him off his feet. Doris wasn't the mastermind behind all of this. She was simply desperate to do her husband's bidding, fearful that Miles would leave her if she refused. Which meant that Miles was the one who had been calling all the shots in this charade. And playing the milquetoast husband to keep the attention away from himself.

"Then don't just do it to save Josie," Noah told her, feeling sympathy for Doris for the first time since meeting her. "Do it for yourself. You don't deserve to be used or ignored by your husband, depending on his whims. No spouse does."

Noah slid the phone across the table to her. "Call the sheriff's office and ask to speak to Deputy Booker. Tell him you've made a big mistake. You and I both know that Josie wasn't trying to steal anything from you."

"Except my husband," she said softly, her lower lip quivering.

He shook his head. "Josie has no interest in Miles. Especially now that she knows he's a liar."

Doris didn't deny that fact about her husband. She'd probably been lied to more than anyone else. "Just make a phone call. That's it?"

"That's enough. Even if you or Miles tries to reinstate the charges later, the sheriff's office won't waste their time. And a prosecutor wouldn't touch this case without a reliable witness. Besides, Josie is planning to leave Calamity as soon as all of this is settled."

"That sounds good to me," Doris said with a snort. "As far as I'm concerned, the sooner she's out of our lives, the better. Josie's been nothing but trouble for us since the day she showed up on Loretta's doorstep like some stray cat."

Noah dialed the number, swearing softly under his breath when the operator told him that Deputy Booker was unavailable. Settling for a junior deputy, he handed the phone to Doris, who performed her part to perfection.

Then she hung up the phone. "You got what you wanted. There are no more charges pending against Josie." She held out her palm. "My money, please?"

He handed it over without complaint. Noah was glad she had taken his first offer, because he would have gone as high as five thousand dollars. "And just in case you change your mind, I've recorded our entire conversation, so the police won't believe you if you try to press charges against her again."

Her perfect brows drew together in outrage. "That's not fair." She catapulted across the table, trying to grab him by the front of his shirt. But she missed, falling over the other side of the table. Her long legs flailed wildly as she hoarsely shouted obscenities at him. She even tried to aim a kick right at Noah's face, but he stepped out of the way just in time.

Doris shot up and ran for the door, but another man blocked her path.

It was Deputy Trey Booker, with Josie right behind him.

Doris pointed a shaky finger at Noah, her voice unnaturally high. "That man forced his way into my home and attacked me. I'm a married woman and he..."

Booker scowled as he looked over at Noah. "Is this true?"

"Seriously?" Noah shook his head. "I came over here to ask Doris to drop the charges. If you call your office, you'll find out she did just that. And I'm sure the person who took her call will say Doris did not sound as if she was under duress."

Josie rushed to his side, looking thoroughly baffled and beautiful. "Oh, Noah, are you all right?"

"I'm fine." He pulled her into his arms, inhaling her sweet scent.

But their hug was short-lived when they heard a roar of indignation from Doris. They both turned around to see her barreling toward the deputy at full speed, trying to get past him. But Trey deftly grabbed her by the wrist and pinned it behind her back.

"I think you need to simmer down, Mrs. Dooley." The deputy placed her in handcuffs. "I'm going to have an officer take you outside to get some fresh air, because the last thing you want is assault charges filed against you."

Josie watched a young female deputy escort a deflated Doris to the front door and usher her outside.

"Miles is involved in this too," Noah said to Trey. "He played the role of the henpecked husband to perfection, making his wife look like the villain to take the focus off him."

Josie sighed. "I think he was convinced that Loretta disinherited him in favor of me." She shook her head, aware of how disappointed Loretta would be by her great-nephew's behavior.

"Is that really what this was all about?" Trey asked.

"Yes," Josie said." I believe Miles was hoping to do one of two things. The first was to find that new will and destroy it, so he'd inherit her estate by default. And if that didn't work, he wanted to get close enough to me that I'd agree to share the inheritance with him."

Trey whistled low. "Amazing."

"It also explains why Miles presumably disappeared without a trace for a few weeks," Noah added. "He probably needed time and space to set up his crazy plan."

"There was another issue too. Doris truly loves him." Josie bit back a sigh, almost feeling sorry for the woman. "The longer Miles was gone; the more desperate Doris was to get him back. That's why she was willing to do almost anything to keep him happy, including kidnapping my cat. I believe he planned all of this, starting the day of Shawn and Amber's wedding."

Trey cocked his head to one side. "You think Miles orchestrated Doris stealing your cat?"

Josie nodded. "It never made sense that she just appeared out of nowhere. But if Miles had been following me and communicating with her, that would make it much easier to pull off such a crazy stunt."

"It probably also explains why she disappeared so easily during the car chase," Noah added. "Miles could have been directing her where to go."

"But why go to all that trouble?" Trey asked, looking perplexed.

"It has to be about the will," Josie mused. She

closed her eyes, remembering those bittersweet final days with Loretta. Josie had loved spending time with her and playing games together until almost her last breath.

She opened her eyes, hit with a sudden realization.

"What is it?" Noah asked, noting something different about her.

"I think I just figured out where Loretta hid her new will."

"Are you sure about this?" Noah asked.

"Yes." Josie's heart thudded hard in her chest. Adrenaline had kicked in, and she silently chastised herself for not figuring this out sooner. But maybe if she had, none of this would have happened. Baby wouldn't have been kidnapped and she would be preparing to start her new job in San Antonio.

And she wouldn't have fallen in love with Noah Tanner.

She couldn't think about all of that right now. First, she needed to know that she was right. They headed for the basement, with Trey bringing up the rear. He'd insisted on coming with them, but only after making certain a warrant wasn't necessary.

Doris was now on her way to a holding cell to cool off. Miles was on his way to collect her. According to Trey, the Dooleys had some questions to answer.

* * *

Josie opened the basement door, then flipped on the light switch. As she climbed down the rickety stairs, it took a moment for her eyes to adjust to the dimness of the room. Both Noah and the deputy were close behind her.

Stacks of furniture and boxes towered around them, partially blocking the light coming in through the small windows. The only other source of light were two bare lightbulbs—one hanging above the stairs and the other at the center of the basement ceiling.

Then she looked around the basement, turning in a slow circle until she finally caught sight of the beautifully hand-painted cat carrier. "There it is."

"Where?" Noah asked, his brow furrowed.

Josie walked over to the far corner of the basement and picked up the cat carrier. "The will is in here. In Baby's house."

Now Noah looked even more confused. "I don't get it."

Josie set the cat carrier on top of an antique school desk. "Whenever Loretta mentioned the will, she'd say it was hidden in the house. Sometimes, she'd say it was under the bed. Miles thought she was just forgetful because of her medication."

A smile haunted her lips.

"I remember Miles and Doris flipping over every mattress at Loretta's place in Austin, certain they'd find the will. But when they came up empty, they assumed Loretta hid the will at her house in Calamity." Josie gave a small shrug. "I did too."

The deputy scratched his chin. "But you were wrong?"

"I was as wrong as I could be." She smiled, remembering that Loretta had never spared any expense when it came to spoiling Baby. Which included hiring an artist to make Baby's cat carrier look like an English cottage. "Loretta hid the will where no one would think to look."

"Until now," Noah said, watching Josie.

Josie placed her hand on the cat carrier and held her breath. Then she unlatched the top. When she lifted the lid, the two men moved closer and looked down inside. The interior of the carrier had been painted to look like a cottage-style bedroom. And at the bottom of the carrier was a plush mat.

"Baby meant the world to Loretta, so it makes sense to me now that she'd put her final wishes with her best friend." Josie gently lifted the mat from the bottom of the carrier. Then her heart skipped a beat. "There it is, right under Baby's bed."

Noah whistled low under his breath. "Well, look at that."

A sealed plastic bag lay on the floor of the carrier. Inside was an envelope with neat handwriting on the front that read: *Last Will and Testament of Loretta C. Reid*.

The deputy shook his head. "This is nuts."

The sight of Loretta's familiar handwriting made Josie choke up. Tears filled her eyes, but she was laughing too. Only Loretta would leave a puzzle behind for her to solve. Now she knew Loretta hadn't been hallucinating at all, but just leaving clues. The will was in Baby's house, under the mattress the cat slept on.

Noah came up behind Josie and placed his broad hands on her shoulders. She leaned back into him and closed her eyes, relieved that she would finally be able to fulfill Loretta's last wishes.

"You did it," he whispered in her ear.

Trey held up the plastic bag containing the envelope. "This will has caused a lot of problems for a lot of people. I think you should take it to her attorney immediately."

"Good idea," Josie said to the deputy. "And to avoid any problems, would you please accompany me to Mr. Lewiston's office? Then you can attest to the fact that I did not open the will or alter it in any way."

"Nothing would give me more pleasure." The

deputy turned to Noah. "Do you mind closing up the house after we leave?"

"Happy to do it." Noah picked up the cat carrier. "And I'll make sure Baby gets back to the ranch safely too."

As she followed the deputy up the stairs, Josie glanced back to see Noah cradle Baby in his strong arms before gently placing her in the carrier. There was nothing standing between her and San Antonio now. Except maybe her heart.

Later that afternoon, Noah scooped feed out by the grain wagon. He'd been living alone on this ranch for the past ten years, but he'd never felt so lonely as he did at this moment. Now that Josie had found her cat and the will, she had no reason to stay in Calamity.

Still, he was happy for her. And Baby seemed happy too. He'd left the cat curled up on his living room recliner after she'd devoured a can of tuna.

He looked up from his work, lifting the front brim of his cowboy hat just far enough to wipe the sweat from his brow. Then he saw Josie's Mazda Miata turn into the driveway and head toward him. His heart skipped a beat as he waited to hear the news that he'd been dreading since they'd found that will.

"How did it go?" Noah asked as soon as she'd parked her car and climbed out.

"Better than I expected." Josie walked over to him, her face glowing. "Mr. Lewiston insisted that we open the will right away. He even got Miles and Doris on a Zoom call with us. They were over in Pine City, but Mr. Lewiston didn't want to wait. He saw no legal issues with the will that Loretta had drawn up. He said, in his experience, it was important to notify the beneficiaries as soon as possible."

"Beneficiaries? Plural?" Noah set down his shovel. "Does that mean Miles made it into her will?"

Josie nodded. "Miles was bequeathed three hundred thousand dollars. I think it stunned him because he didn't say anything for a full minute."

"So, he got her money." Noah shook his head. It actually angered him that Miles had been rewarded after he'd behaved like such a jerk to Josie. "I'm not sure he deserves it."

"Actually," Josie said, swallowing hard. "Loretta had a lot more money than anyone knew. Apparently, she was an excellent investor."

Noah studied her beautiful face, which had suddenly gone very pale. "Hey, are you okay?"

"I'm not sure." She sucked in a deep breath. "No one's ever given me one car, two houses, and three million dollars before."

Noah dropped the shovel from his hand. "What?"

Josie looked up at him, her blue eyes wide. “It’s true! I can’t believe it either. I never wanted anything from Loretta because she had already given me so much.”

Noah tried to ignore the sinking feeling in the pit of his stomach. But Josie’s happiness meant everything to him. “So now all your dreams can come true in San Antonio.”

Her brows drew together. “San Antonio? That’s not my dream anymore. I’ve decided to dream bigger.” She hesitated, as if still not certain this was real. “I already spoke to Mr. Lewiston about creating a foundation in Loretta’s name. He said that was the best way to handle charitable donations. For one, the foundation will fund animal rescue organizations.”

He smiled. “Because Baby brought you and Loretta together?”

“Yes, and I’ve always loved animals. I’ve told you how much horse camp meant to me. The foundation will also direct funds to send foster kids to summer camp.”

The more she talked, the more Noah realized what an amazing woman had hijacked his pickup truck that day. The sun was moving lower in the western sky, turning her blond hair golden in the dazzling light.

“And last, but certainly not least,” she said. “I’m

going to renovate Loretta's home here and turn it into a children's interactive museum. One that celebrates the history of the town and honors the families and communities who built Calamity." She breathed a happy sigh. "There will still be plenty of room for me to live there on the third floor. It will be a mess during renovations, but I don't mind a little dust."

Noah was both stunned and impressed by how much had been decided in the space of an afternoon. "Those are some pretty big decisions in a short amount of time. Do you always spend money this fast?"

She laughed. "Maybe this was my dream all along and that's why it came to me so quickly and naturally."

"Well, I couldn't think of a better place to make an investment," he said honestly. "But all that dust won't be good for Baby, so why don't you two just stay here with me?"

Her blue eyes widened, but he couldn't read her thoughts.

"That's a big decision to make in such a short time," she said at last. "But I don't think I can pretend to be your girlfriend anymore."

"I stopped pretending the day after I met you." Noah took a deep breath, putting his heart on the line like he'd never done before. "I never thought I'd say this to anyone, Josie. But I think I'm falling in love with you."

She took a step closer to him. "I stopped pretending the first time I kissed you. I thought you were a dream that would never come true." Then her voice dropped to a whisper. "Am I dreaming now, Noah?"

"Let's find out." He pulled her into his arms for a kiss. She melted against him as if she belonged there, all soft and warm, but with just enough spice to always keep things interesting. He deepened the kiss, never wanting to stop. She filled every part of him, and he knew, in that moment, that he'd found his forever love.

Long after the kiss was over and they'd both caught their breath, Noah smiled and said, "Speaking of renovations, would you like to see my new hayloft?"

She laughed. "I thought you'd never ask." Josie grabbed his hand and started toward the barn. "Move it, cowboy!"

Six months later

Hives. Dozens of them, covering Noah from neck to waist. Standing only half-dressed in front of the long mirror in the wedding chapel dressing room, he stared in dismay at his reflection.

"This is awful," he breathed, holding both sides of his stiff white dress shirt open for a closer look. The shirt was rented, along with the black tuxedo. Only the Mickey Mouse boxer shorts and socks were his own.

"I agree." Shawn adjusted his tie. "You're about to become a married man. You have to get better taste in boxer shorts."

Noah turned back to the mirror and frowned at his reflection once more. "I can't get married like this. Or worse, go on my honeymoon covered in red welts. It was difficult enough to get Josie to agree to marry me this soon. If she suspects I'm having subconscious second thoughts, she'll make me wait even longer!"

"Calm down and put some of that calamine lotion on those hives." Shawn adjusted his dove-gray vest. "It's worked for you at past weddings."

"No way." Noah set his jaw. "I refuse to wear pink lotion at *my* wedding."

A knock sounded on the door, then Amber walked in wearing a light-blue dress and a big smile on her face "Everybody decent?"

"Somebody here is itching to get married," Shawn told her, grinning. "That's for sure."

Noah shot him a dirty look. "I don't feel like you're taking your best man duties seriously."

Shawn laughed. "Hey, at least I showed up for your wedding ceremony."

"And I'm sorry I missed yours, but I have to say I don't regret it one bit. I wouldn't have met Josie if I hadn't been sitting in the parking lot that day." Noah chuckled. "I guess I have you and Amber to thank for that. If you hadn't set that date to get married and made me your best man, I never would have met Josie."

"You can thank us later when you're helping us build our new deck," Amber told him. "We could use some extra manpower."

"I'll be there," Noah promised, buttoning his shirt.

By the time he put on his jacket and tie, the itchy sensation had increased tenfold. He tried scratching through the fabric of his shirt and jacket, but it proved almost impossible.

Soon after Shawn and Amber left the dressing room, Granny walked in. The jingle of her bangle bracelets preceded her arrival. She wore an emerald-green gown and a big smile on her face. "It's almost time!" Then her gaze fell on her grandson, and she clasped both hands to her chest. "Oh my, you're so handsome, Noah. Just like your late grandpa on our wedding day."

"Thank you, Granny." Noah leaned down to kiss her cheek. She wrapped her arms around him and gave him a big hug.

"Granny," he said, still wrapped in her embrace.

"Yes, Noah, dear?"

"Could you scratch that spot right below my left shoulder blade?"

She pulled back, concern filling her brown eyes as she studied his face. "What's wrong?"

He grimaced, then pulled down the collar of his shirt to reveal the ugly red blotches. "Hives. I think I'm truly allergic to marriage. What if they never go away? I don't want Josie to have to deal with this."

"Don't panic," Granny told him, reaching out to

pat his shoulder. "You're not allergic to marriage. You allergic to eucalyptus."

"What?" Noah cried, confused.

She reached out and neatly plucked the eucalyptus sprigs from his boutonnière. "You were allergic to eucalyptus oil when you were a baby. You used to break out in hives whenever we used a baby lotion with eucalyptus oil in it. But it's been so long ago, I guess we just plum forgot to mention it to you."

"So, I'm *not* allergic to marriage?" Noah asked in disbelief.

"Of course not." Granny tossed the eucalyptus sprigs into the nearest trash can, then she walked over to the sink to wash her hands. "But now I understand why you'd think that way if you broke out in hives every time you were exposed to eucalyptus at a wedding."

Noah shook his head. "I never suspected it was caused by a plant. I just thought it was psychological."

"Well, now you know that's just nonsense." Granny walked over to straighten his tie. "But maybe it was fate, since those hives kept you from marrying anyone until you found just the right girl."

She straightened the boutonniere, now just a lovely red rose with baby's breath, pinned to his lapel. "There. That's much better."

Noah wasn't sure if it was the calamine lotion or

his Granny's healing touch, but he wasn't as itchy anymore. He held out his arm to her. "Are you ready to give me away?"

"More ready than I've ever been." She took his arm and gave it an affectionate squeeze. "Let's get you hitched."

* * *

On the first anniversary of the day they met, Noah and Josie Tanner stood on the front porch of their house on Triple Creek Ranch.

His arms circled around her as they admired the heirloom rosebushes they'd propagated in their flower garden. Josie had gotten the cuttings from the beautiful heirloom rosebushes at Loretta's house in town. She'd recently learned that they'd been passed down through the generations of the Reid family. Maybe even all the way back to Calamity Reid.

"So, what do you want to grow next?" Noah asked, pulling her closer. He'd never felt more at home. "We've got plenty of room on this great big ranch."

"That's true," she said, smiling.

"Bluebells?" he suggested, knowing it was one of her favorite flowers. "Or maybe some blackberry bushes? I can make a hell of a pie."

"Those both sound good, but I have something else in mind."

"Name it," he said, ready to give her the world.

"How about a baby?" She looked up at him with love shining in her blue eyes. "It may take some time, but I think you're just the man I need to make it happen."

He stood dumbstruck for a brief moment, then realized that she'd just given *him* the world. With a whoop of delight, he swung her up in his arms. "We're talking about a real baby, right? Not a cat?"

"A real baby," she said., circling her arms around his neck. "So, move it, cowboy."

He laughed as carried her over the threshold and inside the house. Noah had found his forever love, and he couldn't wait to fill their home with the happiest family in Calamity.

Dear Reader,

Thank you so much for reading *Noah.* If you enjoyed Noah and Josie's story, we would so appreciate a review. You have no idea how much it means to us!

Please look out for the second book in the Cowboys of Calamity, Texas series, *Ben*.

If you'd like to keep up with our latest releases, you

can sign up for Lori's newsletter @ https://loriwilde.com/subscribe/ To check out other books, you can visit us on the web @ www.loriwilde.com.

Much love and light!

—Lori & Kristin

Also by Lori Wilde and Kristin Eckhardt

COWBOY CONFIDENTIAL

Cowboy Cop

Cowboy Protector

Cowboy Bounty Hunter

Cowboy Bodyguard

Cowboy Outlaw

THE COWBOYS OF CALAMITY, TEXAS

Noah

Ben

Will

About the Authors

Kristin Eckhardt is the author of 49 novels with over two million copies sold worldwide. She is a two-time RITA award winner who loves writing romantic fiction. Her debut novel was made into a television movie called Recipe for Revenge. After earning a degree in Animal Science, Kristin and her husband raised three children on a farm on the Nebraska prairie. Along with writing, she enjoys baking, sewing, and spending time with family and friends.

Lori Wilde is the New York Times, USA Today and Publishers' Weekly bestselling author of 97 works of fiction. She's a three time Romance Writers' of America RITA finalist and has four times been nominated for Romantic Times Readers' Choice Award. She has won numerous other awards as well. Her *Wedding Veil Wishes* series has inspired six movies from Hallmark.

Made in United States
North Haven, CT
14 September 2023

41559588R00157